Rorik's Embrace

An Interstellar Alliance Book 1

Judi Lloyd

Rorik's Embrace

ISBN:

All characters, places, and events in this book are fictitious or have been used fictitiously and are not to be construed as real. Any resemblance to actual persons living or dead, actual events, locales or organizations are strictly coincidental.

Dedication

For Mom (1941-2012) and Dad (1937-2023) who both inspired my love of reading and encouraged my love of writing

Acknowledgment

I want to thank my sister and niece for reading the early drafts and giving me advice for the story. Your ideas were wonderful.

Thank you to my family and friends for your words of support and encouragement to follow my dream. It meant the world to me during my days of doubt.

Table of Contents

About the Author

Judi Lloyd is an avid romance reader, crafter, quilter and animal lover.

She spends her afternoons creating make-believe worlds and talking to her characters in her mind. She consumes astonishing amounts of chocolate and pasta and loves to relax by the water. She grew up the third of four children in Michigan, has lived in Missouri and Florida and now resides in Michigan's Upper Peninsula with her husband and two fur babies.

She would love to connect with her readers at judilloydauthor@yahoo.com

Chapter One

Rune stood next to her bed, packing every clothing piece that would fit in a 27" x 21" x 14" luggage bag. Her mother sulked in a chair across the room. "I don't see why you must leave," she grumbled. "You can have children here."

Rune cringed inwardly; they had had this argument once daily since she told her mother her plans. Two weeks ago, she had decided to look for love off Earth. The Interstellar Alliance Program hosted women who wanted something different from Earth. Women paid twenty thousand dollars for a trip to the stars to find a mate. Her mother didn't take the news too well. "I don't want to raise my children alone, Mom. I know you sacrificed everything for me, but I don't want to do that if I don't have to."

In 2320, a plague swept across the planet, killing three-quarters of the male population and one-quarter of the female. The disease killed all those while they slept. Religious fanatics called the plague the End of Days for non-believers, believing that only the sinners had perished. The conspiracy theorists blamed the government for creating and releasing a bio-chemical weapon on the masses. The government, of course, denied all involvement.

Two hundred years after what came to be called The Sleeping Death, marriage is illegal, and procreating is only a business. At eighteen, men must register with one of ten agencies worldwide. Women wishing to have children must certify their fertility before they are allowed to view the male database. Males with a muscular physique or a high IQ can charge higher prices for their services, and the agency adds additional fees depending on the demand for a particular male. The minimum payment starts at around twenty thousand dollars.

Once the fee is received, the males stay with the client until conception. Once the agency-licensed doctor confirms the pregnancy, the agency considers the contract fulfilled, and the male moves on to the next client. This process is the only source of income for many males, enabling many to become extremely wealthy.

Rune knelt in front of her mother. "I want what our people had before the Sleeping Death. I want my children to know both of their parents." She clasped her mom's hands in hers. "I know you love me with all your heart, and I'm thankful for everything you have given me, but I want more for my kids."

Her mother huffed, wiping a tear from her cheek. "I don't trust those other planets. What happens if the male you choose is evil? How will I know? How will you get home?"

"Communication is well-established between the five planets. I'm not sure which one I will choose," Rune replied encouragingly. "Each one has its Pros and Cons about them."

Her mom sniffed. "Don't choose the planet where the males have horns. They look too dangerous." She added with another huff.

Rune looked at her mother strangely. "Does that mean that if I do end up with a male with horns and my child has horns, you will reject him or her?" she asked harshly.

Her mother gasped in surprise at the tone of her daughter's voice. "No! Any child of yours is the child of my heart. I will love it, no matter what. I am just saying to be careful, is all," she said in a softer voice. "You are my baby forever, and I want you safe."

Rune smiled, rolling her eyes. "I'm twenty-five. I'm not a child anymore, Mom," she leaned over, kissing her cheek.

Her mother stood and took a deep breath. "You will always be my baby, no matter how old," she stood, glancing at the luggage. "What do you need me to do to help?" Rune smiled at the truce, and the two women set about packing.

Rune stood in line with the other women waiting to board the spaceship Galaxy, anxious to be on her way. Her mother had stayed with her the previous night. They talked well into the morning about their hopes for the future. Her mother had persuaded Rune to leave her apartment for the year she would be gone. That way, if anything happened off-world, Rune had a place to return.

"How much longer do we have to wait, people? Let's get on with it," a tall blond grumbled loud enough to hear. She stood a good four inches above Rune's tiny five feet two-inch height with an hourglass figure Rune could kill for it. All legs, her blond hair flowed down to her knees, and when she turned, ice-blue eyes stared at her. "Sorry," she mumbled, a blush darkening her cheeks, realizing she had spoken the words out loud.

"No worries," the redhead next to her replied. "All of us feel that way, aren't we, ladies?" she asked the small group. Rune nodded along with the others. The following two months would be exciting, indeed.

"My name is Autumn Fields, and yes, you can laugh at that. My mom had a sense of humor when I came into this world." She looked around at the others. "While we're waiting, let's get to know each other, shall we?" At everyone's nod of acceptance, she continued. "As I said, my name is Autumn Fields. I am twenty years old; I plan on finding a partner in this life on one of the five planets where we will be stopping. Yes, my hair is naturally auburn, and my eyes are naturally this green."

"My name is Skylar King," the blond started next. I haven't looked at the database yet, but I love the planet's name. I am twenty-three years old; I have my eyes on a male from Drakonis. Anyway, yes, I am a natural blond," she finished with a dramatic swipe of her hair.

"My name is Nora O'Brian. It seems I am much older than you ladies at thirty-five. I have tried the male database here on Earth, but the men the agency paired me with were undesirable. Luckily, I realized it before money changed hands. I now want to try my luck off-world. I want to have children, and I'm not getting any younger, so this is my last chance."

"I'm Ruby Reed. I'm twenty, and I'm leaving Earth because of my mother. She wants grandchildren so much that if I didn't leave now, I'm sure she would have me knocked up in months. I caught her hiring a male for his services against my will." She looked at everyone's shocked faces. "Don't get me wrong… I do want kids, but I want them on my time scale and not my mother's," she said with a shudder. "I think my mother would pay someone to rape me until I conceived."

Rune shuddered along with Ruby. "My name is Rune Shadow. I'm twenty-five and want to find love and a mate to help me raise our children. I haven't thought much past that goal."

The ship's ramp lowered, saving Rune from saying anything else. A very tall woman walked down to greet their group. "Good morning, ladies. I am Doctor Ellen and I will be with you for this trip. Our ship, the Galaxy, awaits us just past Earth's atmosphere. The shuttle behind me will take us there. I have been with the program since its conception, and this will be my fifth trip out on the Galaxy. This group is the smallest I have escorted, so I will be brief. The staff has stored your luggage and will bring them to your quarters. Again, this is a small group, so you will each get your room. Once we leave Earth's orbit, I will call each of you to the medical bay for a complete workup of tests for your database. Once done, I will inject each of you with a translator so you can communicate with the population, no matter your chosen planet. So, if you please follow me, we shall depart shortly."

"How long will it take to get to the Galaxy?" Rune asked, suddenly nervous about leaving Earth. The reality of what she was doing hit her hard at the doctor's words.

"It will take about three hours to reach the spaceship," Dr. Ellen answered. "The Galaxy is currently docked at the International Space Station. Everyone will transition to the ship once the shuttle docks at the station. The station has many different observatory areas, including a 360-degree view bay window to watch Earth from the original station in 1998. Go ahead and look, but please don't dawdle too long. We are on a strict schedule and should leave Earth's orbit shortly after everyone is on board."

"Okay, ladies," Autumn started. "Let's say we get to know each other. We have three hours plus months on the Galaxy. It'd suck if we didn't like each other or get along." The other four women chuckled at that as they strapped into their seats.

I'll start," she continued. "As I said earlier, I'm twenty years old. I have a younger, Theo, who is fifteen," Autumn paused for a second before continuing. I also know who my father is. Theo and I have the same parents. Mom chose Dad from the database and fell deeply in love. After his mandatory twenty-year contract, Dad left the agency and returned to Mom," Autumn smiled mischievously. "Theo was born about nine months later." Autumn looked at the others. "I want what my parents have. A love so true it can survive anything. I know I couldn't have that on Earth. Who wants to go next?" she asked the stunned women around her. Except for the very rich, it was very rare to have siblings. To have the same father was exceptionally rare, indeed.

"I guess I will," Rune spoke up. "I am twenty-five and an only child. My mother isn't too happy with me at the moment. She would prefer I stayed on Earth and raised a child just as she did for me, but I want more for my children. Yes, I want more than one," Rune smiled wistfully. My mother is my best friend, but I was always lonely as a child. I had friends, but having a sibling wasn't the same. I want a husband who wants what I desire, to fill our house with laughter and the sounds of many little feet everywhere."

"I have a sibling as well," Skylar stated. "I'm twenty-three, and he's sixteen, though we don't have the same father. We don't have a lot. Mom spent almost everything she had to have us but made sure we knew we were loved. Sebastion, my bruder, is already getting offers from agencies. I've searched the databases in my area and worldwide but couldn't find anyone that sparked my interest. I saw an advertisement for the Interstellar Alliance Program signed up immediately, much to my mother's dismay. She wants her grandbabies around her, not on a remote planet out in space."

"Like I said earlier, I'm escaping my controlling mother's obsession with grandbabies," Ruby said. "I'm also twenty and want to get as far away from my mother as possible, and I plan never to return. My mother is rich and considers me just another one of her possessions. I want a man who sees and wants me, not my mother's money. I dream of having a little boy and girl to shower on all the love I didn't have."

"I guess I'm the granny of this bunch at thirty-five," Nora said with a smile as the other women chuckled and shook their heads. "Seriously, though, I want at least one child, and like Rune, I want the male to help me raise it right. I don't care which planet I find a match on or what the male looks like, whether it has horns, scales, or a tail. I want there to be a spark with whomever I'm with." The other women all nod their heads in agreement.

Rune sat in her room on the Galaxy, her home, for the next two months. She hoped to get along with the other women as they seemed nice. She enjoyed their discussion on the way up to the ship. Those three hours in the shuttle passed by quickly. Nora wasn't what she had expected. At her age, Rune would have thought Nora already had a child. Many women have their babies early to keep up with a small child without help from a male counterpart at a young age. At thirty-five, she was pushing her luck to conceive without trouble or have a smooth pregnancy. She was shorter than Rune by a few inches and had more curves. Her light brown hair hung limply from her scalp as if she didn't care. She wasn't ugly, just plain.

Ruby looked like the fairy tale princess Snow White. Her skin was a porcelain white, and her eyes were the color of milk chocolate. Her jet-black hair cradled her heart-shaped face. Her lips, like her name, were a natural ruby-red color.

She wasn't sure about the doctor. She seemed abrupt in a no-nonsense kind of way. Rune had never seen a woman that tall, at least over six feet, and her facial features, though pretty, looked a little off to be completely human.

"When she said she would fit us with a translator, I didn't think she meant injecting it into my brain," Autumn whined, rubbing behind her ear later that day at dinner. "No warning; just jabbed that huge needle into my head." The other three women nodded and grumbled.

Rune was the last to see Doctor Ellen. "I questioned her nonstop before she could even say hello," Rune sat at the table. "The translator isn't a chip. They're tiny organisms in a clear liquid. They enter your bloodstream and reside in the brain's frontal lobe."

Skylar screeched in shock. "You mean to tell me they put little worms in my brain? Get them out!" she exclaimed, scratching at her head.

Before anyone could do anything else, Nora reached across the table and slapped Skylar on her head. "Stop being a baby. We have many organisms in our bodies, so what's one more? If it helps me understand my future mate, so be it."

Silence reigned over the room until Ruby started giggling. "I like you, Nora. That was great." That opened the floodgates, and everyone began laughing, even Skylar.

The five women settled into a routine over the next four weeks between daily meals, light exercising per Dr. Ellen's orders to combat muscle fatigue in space, and searching the available male databases on the five planets participating in the Interstellar Alliance Program. Skylar only looked at the males from a world called Drakonis. They are a race that is part humanoid and part beast. The males on Drakonis turned into flying raptors resembling dragons from ancient Earth myths. Ruby gravitated toward the database for males on a planet called Katua, where a race of half-humanoid and half-feline beings known as Kotani chose to call home. Other races lived on Katua, but the Kotani were the most prevalent. Autumn believed in the Fates, so she searched all databases and told everyone she would know her future mate when she saw his face. Nora surprised everyone with her choice of males. A minor planet named Ferr is inhabited by a race called Helviti. The world boasted year-round hot temperatures and beautiful beaches. All Helviti sported horns on their heads and reddish-colored skin.

Rune couldn't see anyone she liked in any of the databases. Yes, these males were fine specimens for their respective races, and many boasted wealth and riches on their profiles, but Rune's heart never skipped a beat for any of them. She knew she was being silly, but she wanted what the heroines in her favorite romance novels had. That instant attraction that she couldn't deny. That spark that said, "He's the one." After pleasuring herself with the toy she had brought, she often fell asleep, imagining her new mate.

Jolted awake during a sleep cycle, Rune fell to the floor as the ship rocked onto its side. She rushed into the corridor and found the others searching for the cause of the sirens blaring. Crew members rushed to them, shoving them toward the escape pods. "We're under attack! Slavers!" one man exclaimed, pushing Rune harder. "We have to escape!"

Dr. Ellen waited for the other women at the escape pods. "The escape pods have been programmed with the coordinates to the closest planet in the Alliance. It's Ferr, a three-day journey, so don't be frightened by the length of time in stasis. Each pod has enough power to get there easily. Be safe, ladies, and good luck," Dr. Ellen said as other crew members shoved the women into the pods.

Once the door sealed shut, Rune quickly strapped herself in moments before her pod jettisoned into space. Rune saw the other pods leave the ship before their craft, the Galaxy, was hit with a fire bombardment from another ship five times larger than their craft. Rune prayed that the others could escape, but the Galaxy exploded before the crew deployed more pods. The shock wave blasted outward, sending rocks and ship debris into the life pods. Sparks ricocheted above Rune's head as one system after another shorted out. Fear clutched her heart as her last thought before she passed out was for her mother and her never knowing what had happened to her daughter.

Chapter Two

"I'm not leaving the cabin, Majka. The storm will be here in a few hours, and traveling during a glacial tempest is unsafe. Especially this late season," Rorik tried to reason with his Majka.

"Do not sass me like a youngling, Rorik. I know it's not safe. I wish you had listened to me and your patri. You know I don't like you being at the cabin all alone. What if something happened?"

"Majka, I'll be fine. Bane is here to keep me company and to protect me if the need arises," he soothed the female that presented him. She still treated him and his older siblings, who were thirty cycles old and older, as younglings. Bane, a Wolf-Beast, lifted his head at the mention of his name before lowering it again and wagging his whip-like tail.

"Don't patronize me, Rorik. I may be old, but I brought you into the world…."

"I know, Majka. You have said it since I can remember," he tried a different tactic. "Once the glacial tempest has passed, Bane and I will come for a visit. Will that make you feel better?" Rorik cringed inwardly. He hated going into the city. Ever since the accident, he has been self-conscious about his looks. The town's females gasped in disgust at the scars covering half his face and neck. Children ran from him in fear, crying to their parents, and even his betrothed, Solaini, looked at him with contempt. He could feel the hatred coming off her in waves when they learned of his disfigurement. Her family withdrew her promise to join before he left the medical facility.

"Of course, that will make me feel better. You are my baby, and I want to see you happy. I don't like how you hide away in those mountains of yours. You will never find a good female if you stay up there all the time," his majka admonished. Rorik couldn't find the words to reply. They had had this exact argument for months now.

Ever since he had mentioned that his skin had started feeling tight and the uneasiness he sensed in the quietness of the night, his Majka had declared that his mate was coming to him and that he had to present himself to the masses to meet her. He refused to believe that the Old Gods would bring his mate to him, assuming instead that he was destined to live alone due to his scars.

He looked out the window after ending the call with his Majka. He watched as the white flakes swirled around the ground. He expected another two to three cycles before the storm ceased. He would need to shovel a path to the woodpile in the morning. Turning away, he stoked the fire and added another few logs so the cabin would remain warm throughout the night before heading to bed for some much-needed sleep.

His dreams that night were unlike any he had had before. He didn't want to tell his majka that he had been dreaming of a small female for the past few days. In each dream, she was laughing, but he couldn't see her face. Each time he tried, she moved so her back was always to him. He loved her laugh, light, and carefree sounds that filled his chest with a feeling he couldn't explain but wanted more. Her hair was as black as night, and her skin as white as the flakes falling outside. The dream that night was different, however. He could feel her fear. Something was happening, but he couldn't tell what. He could hear warning sirens in the dream, males and females running in terror. Pain coursed across his body by an unknown force.

A loud boom sounded across the forest hours later, waking Rorik briefly. He stilled, listening to the creatures of the woods or distress from Bane. He laid back down in the quiet. He thought he would need to investigate that noise when the two suns came up before settling back into a slumber. He hoped to dream of the female again. He wanted to know if she was all right.

Rune slowly regained consciousness, immediately regretting it. A whimper escaped her lips as she moved within the pod. The escape pod was only big enough for one person; it resembled an egg-shaped coffin to Rune. It almost was, she thought to herself. The pod's tiny window crystalized with her breath, telling her she might still die if she didn't get out of there and go someplace warm. Tremors racked her body from shock or the cold outside; she wasn't sure, but she had to do something soon, or she would freeze to death. The wind blew through the surrounding trees, whistling with the snow. Rune found an emergency medical kit on the floor at her feet, thankful the Galaxy crew had shown her and the others where everything was in case of an emergency. She just never thought she would need the knowledge.

She pulled out the silver blanket, wrapping it around her head and body the best she could. During the sleep cycle, the attack had happened, and she hadn't thought to wear warmer clothing in the chaos. Her sleep tank and boy shorts would not keep her warm in this weather. Her chest and head hurt, but she didn't have the time to do anything about the pain. She needed to find someplace warm before it was too late. She would rather die trying to find safety than stay where she was and perish because of fear. She took a breath and opened the hatch.

Minutes felt like hours as she trudged through the snow. Within seconds, the snow froze her bare feet. She knew she was in trouble when the snow started looking like a cozy place to sleep. Hypothermia had set in. She struggled to remain standing when she looked ahead and saw smoke rising from a small chimney. Like a mirage in the desert, her greatest wish was before her. Hoping against hope that the cabin existed for real, she slogged through the thick snow, stumbling every few steps. She prayed to whatever God would listen to that the occupant would shelter her for a few days and help her find a way to contact her mother back home.

Rorik had just fallen back to sleep when Bane started barking incessantly. The wolf-beast whimpered before barking again, scratching at the door. Someone here. Someone here, he kept saying in Rorik's mind. Grumbling, he got dressed and came down from the loft. "Quiet Bane!" he commanded, but instead, the animal ignored his master, doubling his efforts at the door. That was when he heard it—a light knocking at the door. Confused about who would be out in the tempest, he quickly opened the door, ready to reprimand whoever was out there.

Shocked, he barely caught the tiny creature as it fell onto the floor. The thing was shaking so badly he could hardly hold onto it. Without thought, he scooped the animal into his arms and kicked the door closed. He laid the creature down on the lounge in front of the fire before turning to stoke the fire. Once done, he returned to the figure. He slowly unwrapped the flimsy silver covering to find a shivering female close to death. She stared at him, teeth chattering. She tried to say something, but he couldn't understand her.

"Quiet female," he tried to soothe her. "I won't harm you. You are safe here." He watched as his words filtered through her mind, and she relaxed. She smiled at him before her eyes rolled back in her head, and she passed out.

Rorik sighed at the unconscious female. This night was not what he had planned. He already dreaded the moment she woke up and saw his face. Would she recoil in fear? Scream and cower in a corner? Looking down at her, he noticed her arms filled with chill bumps. He mentally slapped himself and got to work warming her up. Though pleasing to him, her coverings did nothing to combat the cold. He removed her cold, wet covers as gently as possible and wrapped her in a fur blanket he had made after his last hunt. He saw blood along her hairline and found a small cut, not very deep. He breathed a sigh of relief. He quickly cleaned and dressed the wound before he searched for more injuries. That swiftly done, he gazed down at his unintended guest.

He had to warm the female quickly, or death would take her. He cursed under his breath as he unbuttoned his shirt and pants. Skin-to-skin contact was the quickest way to heat a body. He picked up the tiny creature and placed her on the fur rug close to the roaring fire. He crawled under the thick blanket, her back to his chest. He wrapped his arms around her and prayed to the Old Gods that she would survive the night. Something about her seemed familiar to him. Her body felt right against him, soothing an ache deep within him.

Rune woke slowly with a groan, her body protesting every move she made. Even the tiniest muscle screamed in agony with the motion. She was hot, sweating hot. She moved again, but the groan didn't come from her this time. Rune froze in fear when the weight on her side and stomach moved. She immediately became aware of a large, hard male body behind her.

"Lie still, Little One. Don't worry. I won't harm you," the deep male voice whispered close to her ear, sending shivers down her spine. A moment later, the covers lifted, and the warm body was gone, exposing her body to the chilly air. She was curious about her benefactor but still unsure of her body's reaction to his voice. Nothing had ever made her body respond in such a manner. That fact scared her more than the owner of the voice. Desire pooled in her nether regions, an emotion she had never felt.

She was still deep in thought when the blanket at her front moved. A startled escaped her lips as she quickly backed up against a piece of furniture. A giant dog, more massive than she had ever seen, stood and stretched with a groan. It looked like a wolf from Earth but three times the size. She was two inches over five feet tall, shorter than average for a female, but this creature seemed to be able to look her in the eyes if she stood in front of it, something she didn't plan on doing. She did not want to get up close and personal with those teeth. Thank you very much.

Realizing she was naked, she slowly wrapped the blanket around her. A loud curse sounded behind her. Her body shivered at the husky sound. Her head whipped around, only to find the owner of the sexy voice staring down at her with a frown on his face. Every insecurity she ever had came crashing back to her. She knew she carried an extra thirty pounds around her middle, but she liked the curves the excess weight gave her. Her breasts were more prominent than average; she knew that too. Her DD bras were very hard to find, and even her mother had mentioned that a breast reduction might help her prospects of having children. That was a driving motive for finding love out in the stars. She wanted someone who wanted her for her. If she carried extra weight, then so be it.

Rune watched the male place the logs held at the edge of the fireplace before leaving the room. She blushed in shame at his reaction, and tears filled her eyes in embarrassment. He returned moments later. Seeing her tears, he averted his eyes from looking at her face. She watched as he approached her cautiously.

He was a magnificent shirtless specimen. Over a foot and a half taller than her, his hard, muscled, contoured body, the color of milk chocolate, had her thinking of her favorite dessert. His eyes were so dark, they looked almost black, and his long, silky black hair flowed down to his waist and had her green with envy. She had always wanted long, thick hair, but her black hair was baby-fine and got uncontrollable when it grew longer than her neckline. He reminded her of the ancient gladiators of Rome. The one thing that stopped her breath was the burn damage that covered the right side of his face, trailed down his neck and arm, across half his back, and ended just above his waistline. The scar made his face a perpetual frown.

He knelt in front of her, a blush coloring his cheeks. "I'm so sorry, Little One. I was more concerned about getting you warm last night. I only healed your head wound and checked for broken bones. I should have healed you completely, but I didn't, and I am deeply ashamed." He pulled out what looked to be a handheld scanner and ran it over a deep purple bruise on her shoulder that she hadn't noticed before. It healed in seconds before he moved the scanner to another deep bruise.

Stunned by his actions, she couldn't form any words. His anger had been directed at himself when he saw her bruises, not her whole body. "My name is Rune. What's yours?" she asked when her brain started functioning again.

His smile stopped her heart. It softened the harshness of his scarred face, and the dimple on his left cheek almost shorted circuited her brain again. "I am called Rorik. And that creature is Bane," he motioned to the massive creature sitting beside her. Startled, she jumped back, not realizing he had moved silently toward her. She had been too focused on his yummy owner.

"He won't eat me, will he?" she asked Rorik tentatively. She watched the creature cautiously when he whined and crawled closer before laying his head in her lap. She saw the intelligence in his eyes. Rune looked to Rorik for permission before gently petting the creature behind the ears. The beast immediately rolled over and exposed his belly for her to rub.

Chapter Three

Rorik couldn't believe his eyes. His ferocious, deadly companion had turned into a youngling at the first touch of this female. And what a female she was. Rorik liked her name. He had been clinical the previous night, stripping her coverings and checking for life-threatening injuries. This morning, he was stunned to find her body breathtaking. Curves in all his favorite spots and breasts that could fill his massive paws. He cursed when he saw the bright purple bruises marring her porcelain skin. Now, watching her with his wolf beast, he was struck with recognition at her laugh. This female was his female, the one he had been dreaming about for weeks.

"He likes you," he told her. Realizing he had been staring, he got back to work with the scanner. Once Rorik healed all her injuries, he re-wrapped her shoulders with the fur blanket. He loved her delectable body, but she needed rest. His body wared with that notion. His cock wanted to sink into her warm velvet folds. "I'll get you something to eat." He looked at Bane before he commanded, "Protect."

The damned beast just looked at him, but Rorik heard him in his mind. "Ours. Till death." Rorik grunted and shook his head before heading to the cooking area. He smiled at Rune's shy giggle at whatever Bane had done, and his wolf beast had claimed Rune. Rorik smiled at her quiet question. "Bane won't eat you, Little One, but I just might," he whispered as he set about his task.

Rorik returned to the greeting room to find Bane and Rune playing fetch with one of Bane's many bones. Rune giggled as he placed a wet bone at her feet. Before he could reprimand him for the mess, his mate spoke up. "Good boy!" she praised Bane, roughly scratching behind his ears. "Aren't you such a good boy," she continued before kissing him on his snout. Bane looked up at Rorik, wagging his tail. "Love her. We keep her. Forever. Make her stay. Forever." His companion coaxed. "Claim her. Need her. Want her forever."

Rorik just shook his head. "Meal is served. I hope you like it. It's not much, but it should fill you up."

Rune stood, wrapped the blanket tightly around her, and sat on the oversized couch. "Thank you. For everything." Rorik felt his cheeks get warm with that smile directed at him. He shrugged, unable to say what was really on his mind. He wanted to lay her back on the lounge and dive into her sweet folds until she screamed his name. He ached to plunge into her repeatedly before they both reached their release.

He watched her take the first bite of food. Boar stew was tricky to prepare. Some people loved it; others hated the taste. His cock filled at her moan of enjoyment. He wanted to hear that sound while he was deep inside her. He smiled at her pleasure and dug into his stew. After the meal was done and cleaned, he let Bane out to do his business and start his nightly scan of the perimeter.

He showed Rune where the cleansing room was and how to use the shower before leaving her to get cleaned up. He grabbed one of his thick shirts for her to wear. He was content for her to wear nothing; she was his mate, but he figured she would want something. The coverings she arrived in would not do. They were too flimsy. He laid the shirt on the counter and quietly shut the door, allowing her privacy. Her injuries and need for rest were the only things keeping him from her tempting body.

Rune took her time in the shower. Her thoughts on everything that had happened in the past few days. She hoped everyone had escaped before the explosion, but she knew deep down that some had lost their lives. Saddened by the thought, her mind went to her friends instead. Did they reach Ferr? Were they safe? She sincerely hoped so. Then her thoughts went to her kind rescuer, Rorik. His body was a sight to behold. She imagined what that body would feel like pressed against hers, his lips on her skin. Desire coursed through her body at those thoughts, but she shook her head ruefully. What would a man like him want with a girl like her?

She stepped out of the shower and spied the fresh set of clothes on the counter, smiling as she dried off. Rorik made her heart pound in her chest. Her brain short-circuited around him, especially when he grinned. She sighed. His smile could be deadly to all females, even with his scarring. She pulled the shirt over her head, breathing in his masculine scent. Her lower belly fluttered as the shirt's hem fell to her knees. This feeling is what drove her to travel to the stars. None of the men on Earth nor the males in those alien databases had made her feel this way. Only Rorik.

Bane was back inside when Rune finished her shower. "Thank you. I feel human again."

"Is that what you are? A human?" Rorik asked, stroking Bane's coat dry. The tempest was increasing, and they weren't going anywhere for a few more cycles, at least.

"Yes. I should have asked sooner, but where am I? What planet? I was on the spaceship Galaxy with the Interstellar Alliance Program when the slavers attacked us. The life pod was supposed to land on Ferr, but I know this isn't it."

"You are on the planet Dradus Prime. I know the planet Ferr, but it is a twenty-cycle journey from here."

Rune frowned. "What is a cycle here? Where our ship was in space was a three-day trip in the pod."

Rorik thought about her question. He never had to explain it before. Everyone knew what a cycle was. "A cycle is the time the planet takes to complete one rotation on its axis." He watched Rune for any confusion. He sighed at her nod.

"That's similar to what we call a day on Earth. So, you're saying it will take twenty days to reach Ferr." He nodded his agreement, pleased with her quick mind. His betrothed, Solaini, hadn't cared about learning or working, for that matter. She had been content to sit around and have servants cater to her every want.

"Is there a chance I can get a call out to the Alliance? I need to contact Earth. My mother needs to know that I survived the explosion. I'm her only child."

"I had promised my majka I would visit after the glacial tempest ended. Hers and my Patri's home is in the capital city, Prale. My family will know who to contact."

Rune gave him the widest smile he had ever seen. It spanned from one ear to another. "Thank you!" She wrapped her arms around him, kissing his scarred cheek. He immediately pulled back, shoving her away. "What's wrong? Did I hurt you? Does it still hurt?" she asked, reaching his cheek again.

"No. Don't touch."

Embarrassment heated her face, and tears welled in her eyes. "I'm sorry if I insulted you. I won't touch you again, I promise," she stammered, sitting on the far side of the lounge.

Rorik looked at her in disbelief. She thought he was insulted? Shame coursed through him at the look of devastation on her face. He had put that look there with his actions. He thought back to her touch. He hadn't seen pity or disgust in her eyes, only happiness at first, then curiosity.

His feet moved without thought until he stood before her. He held her tiny hands in his, a look of regret on his face. "I am the one to apologize, Little One. No one has voluntarily touched me or my scars since the accident. Most just run away in fear of my look." He placed her hand back on his face, directly on his scar.

"What happened?" she asked. "Will you tell me?"

Rorik shuddered at her soft fingers caressing his hard, scarred skin. "It happened two planetary cycles ago. I was working in one of the family's mines, monitoring the collection of smaras. There was an explosion deep in the tunnel we were inside. The miners and I rushed to evacuate, but a pipe burst overhead, pinning one of the workers on the ground. I stopped to free him, and with the help of another miner, we did. Unfortunately, the second explosion was even closer to our location. I shoved the men into a side access tunnel just as a third explosion shook the mine. I wasn't able to get to the side tunnel in time. The explosion knocked me against a far wall, exposing my right side."

"Was anyone else hurt?" Rune asked quietly as her tears fell.

Rorik only saw compassion in Rune's eyes. He could feel her heartbreak for the pain he endured after the accident. He smiled and gently wiped the tears from her cheeks. At that moment, he was sure she was the one for him, his destined mate. "Minor injuries, only. I was the only one severely injured."

He decided to take a chance. He sat on the floor and slowly pulled Rune into his lap. To comfort her or himself, he didn't care as long as she allowed it. He breathed a sigh of relief when she nestled onto his lap, then silently groaned as she wiggled her sweet ass a little to get comfortable. He remembered too late that she wasn't wearing anything under his shirt.

To get his mind off his swelling member, he asked her questions. "So, tell me, why were you heading to Ferr? A vacation?"

Rune became fascinated with the hem of the shirt. "Not really," she said, then she sighed. "To understand why I was heading there, I need to tell you a little about my planet," she started. "My planet is called Earth, and a few hundred years ago, a virus swept across the entire surface. Now we call it the Sleeping Death, but almost three-quarters of the male population and only about a quarter of the female population died in sleep. There are so few males now that the government declared marriage illegal, and having babies is now a business transaction." She explained further at his look of confusion. "Females pay the males money in exchange for getting them pregnant."

Rorik thought about her explanation. He didn't know what marriage was or the word pregnant. "Marriage, is that like mates? I don't know the term pregnant."

Rune thought about another explanation. "If mates are two people who promise to love each other until the end, then yes. Being pregnant means being with a child, conceived."

Rorik frowned. "Females pay males to do this? Then what? He leaves her and his offspring?" He growled at her nod. "You wanted this?" his voice elevating in his anger. He would not allow his mate to do such a thing.

Rune shook her head. "No. Many women, yes, that is what they do. That is how my mom had me. She paid a male to have sex with her until she conceived me, then he left." She moved so she faced him. "I don't want that for my children or me. I want a male to stay with me and help raise our kids. That's why I was on the Galaxy. It stopped at each of the five planets so we, myself and the other women on board, could hopefully find true love. Ferr was the first planet. I want a better life than what my mom had when she raised me. So, I paid the Interstellar Alliance Program to take me to the stars so I could find someone to love and who would love me back." Rune suddenly lowered her head and blushed. "Now, I guess that sounds silly." She mumbled.

"No, that's not silly at all," he replied, delighted at her explanation. His finger gently raised her chin to see her beautiful pale green eyes. He cautiously lowered his head and allowed her to lean back if she didn't feel the same. "If you don't want this, say so now." He said, a breath's touch away from her lips. Her silence gave him the permission he needed to touch her lips tenderly.

Rune closed her eyes; she couldn't believe he was finally kissing her. It was her first real kiss from a male. His lips touched hers softly, caressing, questing, just long enough so she could feel the warmth of his skin, and then he was gone. The warmth of his palm caressed her cheek, and his lips were back on hers. Not with the innocence of that first kiss but hot, passionate, and demanding. His tongue pressed against the seam of her lips, urging her submission, which she gave eagerly.

His tongue delved deep into the moist warmth of her mouth, searching, tangling with her tongue in a dance of seduction. Rune's fingers curled into the shirt on his chest as his other hand played with her hair and held her tighter, pulling her closer. He had caught her in his web of desire, a web she didn't want to escape. Rune's hands shyly worked their way up to his broad chest, feeling every crevasse, each muscle on his physique, before she clasped her hands around his neck. Her tongue danced with his, tentatively at first, before becoming bolder with her desire,

With a groan, Rorik's hand ventured from her cheek over her curved body and around to her breast. Its weight held firmly in his palm. His fingers brushed her erect nipple and pinched it roughly as Rune gasped at the slight sting. Breathless from the kiss, she looked into his eyes.

Rorik leaned down, and their foreheads touched as he tried to control his rapidly beating heart and calm his ragged breath. "I've wanted to do that all day," he whispered before showering her neck with soft, gentle kisses.

Rune tilted her head slightly, loving the heat left by his lips on her skin. "You are so out of my league," Rune whispered back, neither wanting to break the spell the kiss had created. Bane ended the sweet moment with a cold nose to her ear and a long tongue across her cheek. She squealed, jerking away from Bane's muzzle, laughing at the creature's wagging body.

Rorik chuckled at his companion's exuberance. "He wanted to kiss you too." He squeezed her hips, not allowing her to move far on his lap. He enjoyed the feel of her body close to his. He felt the heat from her core through his sleep pants.

"Yes. Kiss. Make ours." Bane answered in Rorik's mind. He let out a short yip for Rune and sat down, his tail whipping across the floor.

Rorik shook his head at the animal, scratching him behind his ears. For Bane, life was simple. Everything came down to his basic needs. He only needed a few things to be happy. Had he been happy? Content? Rorik thought back before his accident and his betrothed Solaini. At the time, he believed they were in love, but after the accident, he realized she didn't care about him. She had only wanted his family's credits.

He looked at Rune, her smiling face beaming at Bane as she stroked his fur, content to remain on his lap. His family's business is mining the planet's Samra stones. Samra stones are prized gemstones found deep within the planet's core. Different regions contain colored Samra stones; the StoneBlade Clan owns over half of the planet's mines. Solaini had wanted the power and prestige that came with being a StoneBlade. She desired his name. She didn't like him, at least not after the accident. He wondered what Rune would think about his family's credits.

Chapter Four

"Rune to Rorik, come in, Rorik," a hand waved in front of his face. Rune giggled as his eyes focused back on her and Bane. "Why did you space out on me? Where did you go?"

Rorik frowned. His cheeks blushed at being caught. "What is spaced out?"

"It means that your mind was somewhere else," she replied. "So, where was it? What were you thinking a moment ago?"

"I was thinking about my ex-betrothed, Solaini, and how she is so much different than you." Rorik thought about his answer. He didn't want to cause Rune any stress, but he didn't want to hide anything from his mate. He decided it was best to tell her the truth.

Rune's smile disappeared immediately, replaced by a frown. Rorik continued, not looking at her. "Solaini was from a family that entertained the same areas as my Majka and Patri. Her family and mine agreed that it would be a beneficial match for us to mate. After the agreement, I came to care deeply for her over the next few planetary cycles. Then the accident happened." Rorik paused and looked at Rune's downcast eyes. He cupped her chin and raised her head to gaze into her eyes. "She was nothing like you. You are a far better person than she could ever be," he said before gently kissing her lips.

"What happened?" Rune asked quietly.

Rorik's smile held bitterness, making it more of a grimace. "I was lying in the medical bed, in extreme pain. My family was in the room with the healer when Solaini walked in with her Majka and Patri. The healer told us they had done everything they could for me, but the damage to my body was too extreme. They could do nothing to stop the scarring on my body. Solaini snarled in disgust at my injuries before stating she couldn't be with someone so horribly scarred. She had an image to protect. Her family withdrew the request to mate that night."

"What a bitch," Rune said. "She left you when you were at your lowest. How could she have done that?"

"I found out later that she only wanted to mate with me for my name. She didn't want me." He tugged her closer to his body. "She is now mated to one of our competitor's sons."

Rune smiled and wiggled to get even closer to him. "And now you have me," she said. She wrapped her arms around his neck and pulled him down to her lips. This kiss was just as explosive as the first, and they parted, both breathing heavily.

Rorik touched her forehead with his. "I want you," he said. "I want to take you to my bed and join with you. Will you allow me?"

Rune bit her lip, eliciting a groan from Rorik. He was asking her to have sex with him. Fear and uncertainty flooded her mind. He sighed at her hesitation. "We don't have to if you don't want to. I know my body isn't nice…" his words stopped with her finger pressed against his lips.

"My hesitation has nothing to do with your looks. Your body is perfection." Rune blushed; her entire face heated up in embarrassment. "I want to have sex with you. I wanted to join, but I've never done it before. I mean, I'm not a virgin," she stammered hesitantly. "I don't have a hymen anymore; I took care of that long ago. I have toys I use…" his finger pressed against her lips. She looked down at her lap, mortified.

"Look at me, Rune," he said, waiting for her to obey. He continued when she finally looked at him. "Are you telling me your pussy has never known a male?" He groaned at her shy nod.

"I don't want to do anything wrong. I don't want to disappoint you," Rune whispered with tears in her eyes.

"Sweet Rune, you could never disappoint me," he said. Then, with Rune still in his arms, he quickly stood, eliciting a startled squeak from her. Her arms went back around his neck as he made his way to the stairs leading to his loft bed. "Bane, guard," he commanded, his eyes never leaving hers.

Bane gave a happy bark before curling up in front of the fire. "Make her ours. Make her stay.

Rorik growled at him as he walked up the stairs. He laid her down on his bed and then stood staring at her magnificent body. "Raise your arms over your head," he commanded and watched as she obeyed instantly. He groaned as his covering rode up her hips, giving him a peek at the nest of dark curls that hid her female core. His fingers itched to caress her body, but he fought for control. He needed to see all of her. His eyes darkened with desire. "Remove your coverings, Rune."

Rune shivered with anticipation and excitement. She couldn't believe she was in bed with the sexiest man she had ever seen. His scars only added to his perfection in her eyes. He was masculinity personified. She took a deep breath before reaching down and removing the shirt over her head. Her nipples beaded in the cool air as she watched his eyes stare at her breasts. They ached for his touch. She reached up, massaging her breasts for him, pinching her nipples. She heard his breath catch, and his deep growl thrilled and terrified her equally. She had no idea what she was doing, but Rorik seemed to like it.

"You are the most beautiful female I have ever seen."

Heat spread across her body at the compliment. It pleased her, created butterfly flutters in her belly, and suddenly made her extremely shy. She crossed her breasts self-consciously.

"No," he moved her arms away from her body. "You are stunning, and you will not hide from me. Arms up over your head again, my sweet." Rorik traced her body. He went to his knees. Starting at her ankles, he trailed light kisses up each leg, skipping her mound before continuing across her naval as if he committed every curve, every dip to memory with his mouth.

He smiled at her giggle as he nuzzled the softness of her belly, slowly moving upward to her large breasts. He cupped each one in his palms and massaged them as he burrowed his face into their lushness. She gasped in shock when his mouth latched onto one entire breast and sucked it deep into his mouth. The other breast he pinched, pulled to just the point of pain.

"Rorik!" she screamed, gripping his biceps. He ignored her, entirely focused on the feast before him. He had never felt anything so soft, so giving, and was sure that was how a female's body should feel. The few times Solaini had allowed him to touch her, she had felt thin, bony—nothing like his Rune.

He released her nipple with a pop, then turned his attention to the one red from his rough treatment. His mouth lavished one breast with his tongue, soothing away the pain while his fingers tormented the other. The kaleidoscope of feelings had her fingers digging into his scalp, groaning in pleasure.

Rorik gripped her thighs, slowly pushed them apart, and settled between them. He wanted nothing more than to plunge into her hot core until they both cried out in release, but he couldn't. Not just yet. He was her first, and he was honored by her gift. He needed to prepare her for him. First, he would give her pleasure.

"I can smell your desire, sweet Rune," he said against her naval. "Tell me, do you want this? I can stop now if you want, but I can't be certain for a few more moments. Tell me, what do you want?"

"I want this," she gasped as she gripped his hair. "I want you." Nothing else mattered in her mind.

He growled his answer into her soft belly. He moved lower, his hands massaging her upper thighs, easing her tension. He inhaled her unique scent; his thumbs tenderly parted her curls, revealing an unimaginable treasure. Unable to wait longer, he lowered his head and tasted her sweet juices.

Rorik groaned in ecstasy. She was sweeter than a beltza berry during the summer heat. He separated her lips and continued to explore her folds. He found her nub and latched on.

"Oh, God!" Rune screamed; her head fell back. Her hips reflexively jerked upward. She had never felt anything like this before. It felt amazing.

Rorik grabbed her hips and pressed her down into the resting mat, never ceasing his attack. He slowly dragged his rough tongue across her folds as he lapped up her juices. Her flesh trembled in response. She could feel his fingers dig into her flesh; she would have bruises tomorrow.

"Please, Rorik…" Rune couldn't help but beg even though she didn't know for what. Rorik slowly pressed one finger into her slick opening and found it unimaginably tight. He groaned as her velvet walls tightened even more around his digit. He pushed in further before withdrawing. She whimpered in denial at the sudden emptiness but cried out when he pressed two fingers into her channel. He slowly moved in and out, scissoring his fingers as he stretched her.

"More," she gasped, her hands gripped his hair, pulled slightly. "I need more," her head tossed side to side. Rorik loved the tiny pricks of pain caused by her pleasure. He obeyed her command and increased the speed of his fingers. He lightly sucked on her small nub, and she screamed. Her back bowed so only her shoulders and hips remained on the mat as a powerful orgasm slammed through her body.

Breathless, Rune lay there on the mat, weak as a newborn. She just had her first orgasm made by an alien male. It was everything her romance books had said and even more so. She looked down at Rorik.

While she was dazed, he removed his clothing and was now at her entrance. "Wait!" she tried to pull away from him. He growled, his face a mask of primal desire. "You're too big!" She attempted to back away.

The fear in her voice softened his stance, but he didn't release her legs. He eased them apart, then leaned forward, his hands on either side of her head. He kissed her gently. "It will fit," he said softly as he slowly pressed the head of his cock into her pussy. Her orgasm had made her slick, but she still struggled to accept his engorged head. "You are so tight," he groaned, trying to control his desire. He gave a quick, small thrust that allowed his head to enter. At her gasp, he halted, his body drenched in sweat from the strain.

He leaned farther down and sucked a nipple into his mouth. Rune gasped at the new sensation, distracting her for a moment. Rorik withdrew slightly, then pressed in a little farther. He continued his shallow thrusts, and with his distracting mouth, they soon rested hip to hip.

He looked into her eyes. "Are you okay?" It would kill him, but he had to stop if she was in too much pain. She was his mate, and her needs came first.

Rune looked into his eyes and saw concern for her and her pleasure. It humbled her that he would stop and ask about her, even when she knew he desperately wanted to continue. She smiled. "I feel full, stretched, but no pain." She rotated her hips to encourage him to resume.

He groaned at the movement; his legs trembled. "I can't control it anymore," he growled.

"Then don't," Rune replied, rotating her hips again. "I want everything, and I want you."

Rorik swore under his breath and thanked the Old Gods for bringing her to him. She was so small, but her words encouraged his body to let go of his control. With a loud growl, he withdrew almost entirely before slamming back into her. He continued the rhythm of slowly retreating and powerful thrusts, increasing the tempo with each thrust. "So good. So tight. So good," she could hear him murmur under his breath like a mantra, his head buried in the hollow of her neck. She briefly wondered if he could breathe.

He pumped into her even faster, as his life depended on his release. He clutched her tight, close to his chest, as if desperate.

Rune wrapped her arms and legs around his body and hung on. His unbridled passion had her gasping in pleasure. Her breasts bounced as he continued to plunge into her. He was large. More significant than any of her toys back home. He hit places deep inside she never knew were there. Pleasure began to build up in her belly. A liquid pleasure turned into molten lava. Her legs shook, and she screamed out louder than ever before as the orgasm shattered her soul in its intensity. The world stopped spinning briefly, and everything was still except the fireworks coursing through her body.

On the tail of her climax, Rorik ferociously pumped a half dozen more times before he stilled. He pressed into her as deeply as he could and roared his powerful release, coating her womb with his seed. He lazily thrust in and out a few more times to prolong her pleasure before finally coming to a halt, still inside her body. Their ragged breaths were the only sound as their hearts slowed back to normal. Her body still pulsed with aftershocks.

Rorik raised his head from her neck and gently kissed her lips. "I should apologize. That was the last thing you or your body needed after last night's ordeal." He kissed her again, more forcefully, to stop her from arguing. He brushed her hair away from her eyes, suddenly glassy from unshed tears. "I should apologize, but I won't. I can't. That was amazing, and I refuse to apologize."

Rune smiled through her tears. At first, she thought he was disappointed that she hadn't satisfied him. But no, he was worried about her. "I don't regret a thing," she said, fingering his hair. Before she could speak another word, a huge yawn escaped. "I'm sorry," she stated, her cheeks pink.

Rorik smiled and kissed the tip of her nose before slowly pulling out. They both groaned in response. He maneuvered them into the middle of the mat and covered them with fur blankets. He tucked her close to him, her back to his front, and breathed in the smell of her hair. "Sleep now, sweet Rune," he whispered in her ear. "Tomorrow is a new day." She didn't reply, but he listened to her breathing even out.

He lay there for hours listening to her breathing. The Old Gods had deemed him worthy of a mate. His mate! Until last night, he had never rested with anyone before. He couldn't believe she could trust him so easily. He silently vowed to the Old Gods to do everything he could to protect his mate and keep her happy. With that thought, he slipped into slumber.

Chapter Five

Rune slowly woke up. Her muscles deliciously ached from the previous night's activities. She smiled at the thought. Last night was nothing like she could have imagined. Everything exceeded her expectations. She could hear the wind whipping outside, the blizzard still strong. She wondered how much longer it would last. How long until she could contact her mom? She heard Rorik arguing with Bane downstairs and giggled. He talked to his Bane like the beast understood everything. She stopped for a moment and considered that fact. Now that she thought about it, they acted like they were having silent conversations several times yesterday. She shook her head but stopped and shrugged. Anything was possible.

She searched Rorik's closet and found another long shirt to wear. She located a pair of sleep pants that wouldn't stay around her waist. Deliberating momentarily, she left the pants on the mat and searched for food.

"Make her ours. Make her ours," Bane insisted as he growled at Rorik.

Rorik growled right back, stirring the food on the stove. "We can't make her ours, not yet anyway. I want her to stay just as much as you do, but it has to be her choice. I need to explain how important mates are here. I have to find a way to tell her she is my fated mate," Rorik argued. "You know how it works; she must agree before we speak the ritual words."

"She agrees later. I want her now. Make her ours now," Bane argued like a youngling. He didn't care about the repercussions; his only instinct was to protect what he considered his family, and Rune was his.

Rune listened to Rorik's side of the argument. She frowned at the mention of mates and fated mates. What was the difference? Why did he think they were fated? Before Rorik could continue his argument, she walked into the kitchen area. "Why do you think we're fated mates?" she asked, surprising them both.

Rorik stared at her like an animal caught in a set of headlights. Shock and fear, as well as other emotions, crossed his face. She smiled as his eyes darkened with desire as his eyes raked up and down her body. She had chosen a shirt the same color as her eyes. Her smile widened at his growl when he realized she wasn't wearing anything underneath.

Rune sat at the small table by the wall. Bane stood beside her, placing his massive head on her lap. "Well?" she asked, looking at Rorik.

"You're ours." She heard a voice say in her head. Rune's eyes widened as she looked between Rorik and Bane.

"Who…who said that?" she asked quietly, looking around the room. Rorik sighed and placed his head in his hands. Bane whined in her lap.

He sighed and resigned to explain things to Rune before working out a plan, shutting off the burner, and sat opposite Bane. He didn't want to distract himself from her gorgeous curves. He almost swallowed his tongue when she walked into the room. She filled out his coverings much better than he did.

"What did the voice say?"

Rune licked her lips. It said, 'You're ours.'" She looked around the room, absently petting Bane's head. He whined, and she looked down at him. He stared up at her with devotion in his eyes.

"Bane said that," Rorik said. "I need to explain many things, but first, how about some food?" he babbled, returning for the food.

"I could eat. Our activities last night made me very hungry," she smirked. She laughed at his hungry growl. "I want more playtime, but first, we must talk." Rorik nodded and silently served the first meal for the three of them.

After cleaning up, they sat on the couch, and Rune faced Rorik. "Okay now, first things first," she said. "How can Bane speak to me in my head?" she asked, watching Bane curl beside the furniture.

"To answer that, I need to tell you about my family and our culture," he replied. He took a deep breath to calm his nerves. She was his everything, though she didn't know that just yet. This conversation would make or break their relationship.

"In the StoneBlade Clan, as well as others, it is customary that all members, male or female, somehow contribute to the family business. For the males, that means working in the mines, sometimes deep within the mines," he waited for her to nod before he continued. "The males start working in the mines at around ten summers old. They are old enough to understand the importance of their task but still small enough to traverse some tighter tunnels without trouble. In their eighth summer, they participate in a ritual bonding ceremony that bonds him to his protector."

"What happens at this ceremony?" she asked. Stroking Bane's head, which once again rested in her lap.

"The ceremony matches the youngling males with a young wolf-beast or animal of their own as their protector."

"So then, you chose Bane to be your protector?"

Rorik smiled at his companion, "No, the wolf-beast chooses the youngling, not the opposite. The children stand in a giant field surrounded by a forest. The Eldar, one of the oldest males on our planet, conducts the ceremony from a large dais. He chants a blessing in an ancient tongue, calling all young beasts to choose. The children stand perfectly still until the animal accepts the child and nuzzles his palm. Then, the child may touch the animal, but he must keep his eyes closed until the Eldar closes the ceremony with another blessing. Once the animal chooses, that is it. Animal and child bond for life."

"Anyway, after the ceremony, the youngling and the wolf-beast are inseparable. Animals and children gain each other's trust through their actions over the next two planetary cycles. After that, they are sent into the mines to work for the next eight planetary cycles. Once finished, they move into other roles in the business as needed."

Rune's face paled at the thought. "Was Bane with you at the accident?" she looked down at the animal, searching for signs of injury.

"Yes and no, he was with me in the mines, but I told him to protect the men in the tunnel. He wasn't with me during the explosion." He pulled Rune into his lap when he saw her tears. "I'm okay now," he soothed her, wiping away the drops with his thumb.

"But you're not okay. You're in a cabin, alone with Bane, on the side of a mountain. You're nowhere near your family."

Rorik smiled. Her compassion filled his heart with love. "I'm right where I should be. I saved you, didn't I?" he said. She nodded, gracing him with a tearful smile.

"To continue, the ritual allowed us to connect telepathically. I can hear Bane's thoughts in my mind, and he can hear mine if I communicate that way."

"Okay, I get that, but how can I hear him? I didn't go through a ritual," she said. She rested against his shoulder. Rorik smiled into her hair, taking a deep breath. So far, she had accepted him and Bane. He loved her mind and her thought process. She impressed him with her questions.

"That, combined with how I've felt since I found you, is why I think we are mates. Fated Mates, to be exact." He held his breath and waited for her refusal. When she just stared at him, he slowly continued. "With mates, the attraction takes time, sometimes planetary cycles. It gradually builds up over a long period. Over that time, if the bond is strong enough, the mates develop a mind link. But with fated mates, it is much shorter, sometimes instantaneous.

"You're talking about love at first sight." She said, turning quickly in his lap to face him. He saw the excitement shining in her eyes. Her smile lit up the room at his nod. "On Earth, that was an old saying before the Sleeping Death. People would say it was 'love at first sight when they met their partner.' I've read about it in old books." She suddenly looked at him, confused. "Do you think that's what's between us?"

He couldn't help but smile. Rune's willingness to believe in being a fated mate almost brought tears to his eyes in relief. "She agrees. She likes us. Make her ours now." Bane spoke up in his mind.

Rorik rolled his eyes. "Not yet. She still needs to understand. Soon, I promise," Rorik answered, using his mind this time. He didn't want Rune to know of this conversation just yet.

"Yes, I know that is what it is. Tell me what you thought of me when you first saw me?" Rorik smiled at her pink cheeks. "No, untruth now," he said teasingly.

"I thought you looked magnificent and resembled a picture I had seen of a gladiator from ancient Rome back on my planet." She blushed even more at his look of confusion. "You have a gorgeous muscled body, a small tapered waist, and big hands and feet. Honestly, even your scars are sexy to me."

"What do my hands and feet have to do with anything?" he asked, a confused frown marring his face. He didn't want to talk about his scars, but his cock stiffened with Rune's confession. To him, his damage was hideous, not sexy.

We watched as Rune's cheeks turned an even brighter pink. "It doesn't matter," she deflected. "Your turn, answer the same question."

Rorik smiled, thinking back. "What I thought when I first saw you doesn't count. You were almost frozen solid when you fell into my arms. That next morning, though," he paused. "I thought that you were the most beautiful creature on this mountain. My heart stopped beating, and for just a moment, I couldn't breathe. When you smiled…" he stopped, a blush coloring his cheeks.

"What?" she asked. She was curious. Her insecurities were flaring to life once more. What didn't he like about her? Was she too fat? Too short for him. Everything worked perfectly last night when they joined.

"When you smiled, you became my world. Then, when you did that cute little giggle at something Bane did, I knew you were the female of my dreams. You are perfect for me."

"Wait, you dreamed about me?"

He hesitated briefly, trying to decide how much to tell her. He realized that he couldn't hold anything back. She was his mate, and she needed to know everything. Once their bond was strong enough, he would be able to feel her emotions as well as read her thoughts. She would be able to do the same. "Yes, I dreamed of you for the last twenty cycles, even the night I found you."

Rune bit her bottom lip, unsure what to say to his confession. She also had a confession, so before she chickened out, she exclaimed, "I dreamt of you too."

Rorik watched her worry her lip. He wanted to nip and soothe it for the remainder of the day, among other pleasurable activities. He was deep in thought at her confession, so it took a few moments to process what she said.

Rune watched the look of shock cross in his eyes before it morphed into amazement and delight. "That proves even more that we are fated mates," he said. His face beamed with pleasure. "It is rumored that fated mates dream of each other before they meet. The Old Gods made it so that the souls of two mates would know each other before their physical bodies met.

He watched her ponder this, feeling her uncertainty. He was astounded that he could sense her emotions. The elders all said that it took time to develop the link. It had barely been a cycle since she arrived. He wanted to test his theory. "I can feel your uncertainty, sweet Rune," he said, kissing her head. "Do you feel anything from me?"

Rune frowned at his words. Could she feel anything from him? What did that mean? Closing her eyes, she took a deep breath and slowly let it out again. She then repeated the process. There, in her heart, she felt something. It was a strange feeling. Excitement, nervousness, and love? That last feeling tugged at her heart. These were not her feelings but someone else's. "You're feeling excited and very nervous," she said as she opened her eyes.

"Exactly!" Rorik said. He devoured her lips in a hungry kiss, and she straddled his body, trying to get closer. He leaned over and pressed her into the couch. His hand went under the covering and grazed her wet and waiting mound. So hot. He could smell her arousal. He stroked a finger across her pleasure nub, claiming her as his own. He would soon claim her in every way. He pulled just a breath away, panting to catch his breath. "I want you. Please, I need to be inside you now."

"Yes," she whispered against his lips. That was all he needed. He pushed his sleeping pants down his legs and thrust into her in one motion. They groaned in unison. His hands gripped her ass cheeks, lifted her off the cushion, and gave him deeper access to her velvet channel.

He held himself still for a moment, allowing her to adjust before pulling out until just the head of his cock was left inside. "Don't stop," Rune sighed as he kissed the hollow of her neck, his cock slowly sliding back inside her waiting heat.

"I've dreamed about you all night. The incredible feeling of this hot, wet pussy surrounding my cock. I almost woke you up a few times last night. Tell me you're mine, Rune," he said, sliding back out. "I need to hear it. Tell me, and I will give you your heart's desire." He drove in with more force as she gasped in response.

Rune was caught up in the myriad of sensations. She could barely perceive the world around her as she thrashed about. Rorik was everywhere at once. His hands had moved to her hips, pinning her where he desired. His thumbs flicked her tiny nub as he stroked in and out of her pussy, building in tempo. The only sounds in the room were of slapping flesh and ragged breaths. Rorik growled, slamming into her heated flesh. "Say it!"

"I'm yours," she whispered. Rune's breath hitched as he increased the pressure on her clit. His strokes became quicker and insistent. It was as if she were an instrument and he a maestro. He stroked her with just enough speed to send her to the precipice. She keened when the pressure backed off.

"Again," he commanded, his muscled taunt from control. "Louder." He needed to hear her voice.

"I'm yours, Rorik!" she shouted as he quickened his pace. She tightened her hold around his neck, her nails digging into his flesh. She eagerly matched his strokes, meeting him, thrusting against him. She felt his body tightening, his expression showing his fight to remain in control. Each thrust bordered on pain, but she wanted more. She chanted his name and the words he demanded that she repeat. Together, they chased their release until one final deep thrust, and she screamed his name. She felt her soul leaving her body to join with his above them, returning before she came beneath him, and he froze above her.

A second later, he pulsed inside her, warmed her womb, and shocked her with another hard orgasm. As he emptied himself into her, her world exploded into a white abyss filled with colorful fireworks.

Rorik looked down at his mate's face and her look of rapture. That was the most beautiful thing he had ever experienced. He smiled and couldn't wait to do it again.

Rune woke up on the couch a few hours later, a fur blanket wrapped around her. She smiled and stretched out her aching muscles. She thought about the earlier conversation and Rorik being sure they were mates. Why was she so uncertain? She had read books that reference that 'love at first sight' feeling. She had traveled to the stars looking for love. Why was she hesitating?

Rune argued with herself with mixed emotions. The first issue, she wasn't even supposed to be on this planet. Once she contacts her mother, she should continue to Ferr. The next problem was that she felt a pull toward Rorik, even Bane. Could she leave them behind? Her stomach rolled at the thought of never seeing her guys again. Her body stiffened at the thought. Wait, they weren't her guys. She mentally scolded herself.

They could be, a mischievous voice said in her head. They're everything you have ever wanted. Rune smiled at that thought. Yes, they were her guys. She loved them both. It was love at first sight. Her mother would tell her it was too early to call the feeling love, but Rune knew better. She needed to talk with Rorik and confess that she loved him and wanted to be his mate. Standing, she remembered their lovemaking and how Rorik had demanded that she be his. Well, he was hers too, forever. Smiling, she went looking for her mate.

Rorik was outside, collecting more wood for the fire, when he felt Rune wake. He could sense her indecision, and it hurt his heart. He consciously blocked his mind so she didn't perceive his emotions. He didn't want to unfairly influence her decision on whether she should stay or leave when the storm ended. He desired her to remain with him and Bane, but he would never coerce her to do something she didn't like. He was a scarred monster, barely a male. His mate deserved better than that, and she deserved better than him.

He shivered in the cold; the fierce wind whipped the frozen crystals into his unprotected face. "Boundary clear. She safe." Bane announced as he bounded back to Rorik's side. "She up. Need her." He insisted as he looked to the cabin's back door.

"Not yet. Rune needs some time to think without us being there," he answered with mind speak. "We must be patient if we want her to choose us." He smiled at Bane's grumbling.

"Rorik? Bane? Where are you?" The male and beast froze, looking at each other and then back at the cabin. "Am I doing this right?"

Rune screeched in surprise when the back door opened, and her guys walked in. She screamed again as he twirled her in his arms. "Rorik! You're covered in snow and ice! Put me down!" She half-yelled and half-laughed at his exuberant return.

He set her down with a passionate kiss on her lips. "Yes, my sweet Rune, you did that right."

Her eyes grew wide in happiness. “You heard me? Really?” she bit her lip with excitement. “Will you try it with me? Say something to me with your mind,” she demanded.

“You are my world,” he said in mind, speak. He smiled as Rune’s smile lit up the cabin.

“I heard you!” she squealed with excitement. “Wait, we never finished our conversation earlier. How can I hear Bane if I didn’t go through a ritual?”

“Since Bane and I connected through the ritual, and you and I are connected by being fated mates, then technically, you and Bane are connected as well through me.” Rorik smiled at her question. Her mind was sharp. He guided them into the living area in front of the fire.

“That is so cool,” she said in awe. “So, do you have to be near for me to be able to mind- speak with Bane?”

“I think so, for now. But when we are officially mated, then no.”

Rune bit her lip and shyly looked between Bane and Rorik. “I need to talk to you about that. You had mentioned mating and ritual words before. What did you mean? What kind of ritual is it? Will there be other people with us?”

Rorik took a deep breath. He couldn’t believe they were talking about mating. “The actual mating ritual is private, done behind closed doors, usually in resting areas. He looked at her face until she understood. She blushed at his insinuation and kept quiet. Adorable, he thought. He wanted to think of other ways to maintain that look on her face.

"When I enter you, I will start the ritual. I will recite the Mating Pledge. I will say, 'You are mine to protect, love, honor, and cherish in injury or not. Until death takes me from you, I am yours. Before the Old Gods, I proclaim you as my mate,'" he continued. "Then you will say those words back to me. We will time our release with your final words. We hold each other close, and the Old Gods will bless our union with a mark on our chests. The stronger the union, the stronger our bond, the closer that mark is to our hearts."

"Once our union is blessed," he smiled a wicked grin. "You will get into the breeding position, and we can start trying for offspring."

"You want kids?"

"Yes," he looked hesitant. "You do want offspring, don't you? That's why you left your planet?"

"Yes, that's one of the reasons I left Earth, and yes, I want kids or offspring," she grinned mischievously. "I want many offspring."

Rorik kissed the tip of her nose. "I will give you everything your heart desires," he said. He hugged her close. "Now, let's talk. Tell me about your Majka."

Rune woke slowly, smiling, stretching her aching muscles. The last four days have been bliss. With the storm still raging outside, Rune and Rorik grew closer. They talked about anything and everything. She laughed at his tales of growing up the youngest of three children. He teased her about being an only child and how lucky and wonderful he thought that was. Rune retaliated because her mother knew who was at fault if she did something wrong. He was the lucky one to have siblings to blame.

Spending this time with Rorik and getting to know him and Bane, she no longer had any doubts. She was in love with Rorik. No doubts, no hesitations. She was in love. She found another of his shirts and pulled it on, taking a deep breath of his unique scent. She could hear Rorik chopping more wood outback. "Rorik," she thought. She liked the silent communication they shared.

"I'll be right in, my Sweet Rune. I can feel your happiness," came his reply. Her heart skipped at his pet name for her. It made her feel like she belonged to him. Not in a wrong way, but more like he owned her love, and she held his.

The object of her affection walked into the cabin moments later and twirled her around. Laughing, she shook her head. "What am I going to do with you?" she breathlessly asked once he set her back down.

"Love me." He said instantly. His eyes grew wide as he realized he had spoken the remark out loud. He looked at her, and the shock on her face turned to excitement and relief.

"I do," she replied. "That's why I'm happy. I love you." She caressed his scarred cheek. Happiness filled her being when he didn't move away from her hand. It was the first time he didn't shy away.

"I love you too," he whispered. He leaned down and kissed Rune's lips gently. "What would I do without you?"

"That's what I want to talk to you about," she started. She rubbed Rorik's arms, and his entire body stiffened at her words. "I want to make sure you never have to know. I'm not going anywhere. Now or in the future."

She smiled at the look of hope in his eyes. "What are you saying, Sweet Rune? You need to say the words," he said, anticipation and excitement shining in his eyes.

"I want us to be mates, true mates. I want us to have many offspring, and I want to start now." She threw her head back and laughed before wrapping her arms around her mate's neck in a bear hug.

She squealed as Rorik scooped her into his arms, giggling excitedly as her mate rushed up the stairs to their resting room.

Chapter Six

"Strip," he commanded. The growl in his voice sent shivers down her spine and moisture to pool between her legs. She eagerly complied; excited goosebumps fluttered down her arms. "Slowly," he growled. His hands fisted by his sides.

She immediately slowed; a seductive smile crossed her face as she bit her bottom lip. She could tell Rorik was fighting himself. His body trembled with exertion to hold himself in place. After what seemed like hours but was only a few minutes, she stood naked before him.

He grabbed a pillow from the sleeping mat and tossed it on the floor. "On your knees." She looked at him strangely but did as he commanded. Protests sounded in her mind. She was an independent woman. She shouldn't obey without question, but her body disagreed. Her heartbeat increased in tempo, and moisture coated her legs. She had read about this in her romance novels. Her body desperately wanted the experience. "Undo my coverings, Sweet Rune." He watched as she struggled with his closures, her hands shaking. Once finished, she looked up and waited for his command.

He looked into her trusting eyes, fearing how Rune would accept his commands. He was alpha. He required control during mating. He had tempered his tendencies in the last few days but couldn't any longer. She needed to obey him to be his mate, and he wanted her to enjoy it.

"Sweet Rune, do you trust me?" he asked.

"Yes," she answered without hesitation.

He smiled at her instant response. "Then suck me," he commanded. "Take me in your mouth and suck me." He grabbed a handful of hair to guide her head. She gave a seductive smile as she lowered his coverings. His cock sprang free from its confines and bobbed in her face.

Rune looked at him, suddenly shy. "I've never done this before. I've read about it, however. Will you tell me if I do it wrong?"

Excitement coursed through him. Rorik had forgotten that he was her first. He was her first for everything, it seemed. That realization weighed heavily on his mind. He wanted her to enjoy giving herself to him. "Wrap your sweet, warm mouth around my cock. No teeth. You can't go wrong doing anything else," he stroked her hair to reassure her. "I'll instruct you when needed, my sweet Rune," he added at her look of uncertainty.

That was the reassurance she needed to grasp him in her hand. She required both to wrap around his shaft fully. His cock was rock hard under a smooth layer of skin. The head was soft as she licked the tip before she closed her lips around it.

Gently, she moved her mouth over his shaft, only taking half in her mouth. His hum of pleasure gave her another boost of confidence. As she rolled over his rod again, she felt him stiffen even more than before. His swollen shaft intensified to the point of almost pain in her mouth. She refused to stop. She wanted to please him as he had pleasured her.

"That's good, my sweet," he groaned in appreciation. "Now, use your tongue."

Not entirely understanding what he meant, she thought back to her books. She remembered how the heroines made their men feel and suddenly understood. She teased the underside of his cock with the tip of her tongue, messaged the thick veins with the flat of her tongue, then swirled around the head. She lifted her mouth to lick the tip, tasting the white pearl drop. Taking him into her mouth as fully as possible, she gently sucked her way back to the end.

"That's right, my sweet. Now use your hands," Rorik fisted Rune's hair and gently rocked back and forth. He didn't want to end this too soon. He needed to think about other things to keep his mind off the delicious sensations she gave him.

Hands? She didn't know what he wanted. She had her hands on him already. She stopped and looked up. Wordlessly, he spread his feet apart, and his balls swayed, attracting her attention. She was curious and had never seen any part of the male anatomy up close.

She slipped a palm under one, lifting, feeling its weight. Her fingers caressed it. Heavy and soft at the same time. Rorik groaned when her nail ran along the bottom. She could tell that he liked what she was doing from their link, but she wanted to drive him crazy just like he did to her.

She licked and nuzzled his balls, breathing in his musk scent before returning her attention to his cock. She licked her way back to the tip, then grasped his thick base with both hands. She took him in her mouth again, sliding over him at various speeds, gliding her hands up and down in contradiction. He grew thicker, harder, almost more than her mouth could take. She squeezed gently, and his leg muscles trembled in response.

She was going to be the death of him. Her hot, moist, eager little mouth and awkward movements only made it worse, keeping his mind entirely on her and what she was doing to him. He groaned as her hands squeezed his stiff shaft again. He gripped her shoulders. "Stop. I'm going to come." His words only drove her movements faster until he shouted his release, spilling his seed into her mouth. She cleaned him up, swallowing everything he had given her. Her tongue swiped a final lick across the tip of his cock, and she shined a bright, happy smile at him.

"You are a very naughty female," he said between heavy breaths. "I never allowed you to give me a release."

Her eyes twinkled in mischief. "Sorry…Sir," she replied in no way repentant.

He helped her stand. "On the sleeping mat with you," he said, slapping her backside. She yelped and crawled onto the mat. He went to his closet, extracted what he needed, and stood beside the mat.

"Give me your wrists," he commanded. Rune stared up at him. Uncertainty was etched on her face. He patiently waited for her to do as he said. She expelled a deep breath before placing her wrists in his hands. "Well done," he stated. The approval in his voice filled her with pleasure.

He secured both wrists with a silk strap, then attached it to the headboard. Rune pulled on the bindings; fear bubbled up. She yanked on the straps again, understanding the vulnerable position she was in now. "Rorik, I don't like this; let me go."

"Rune, look at me," he caressed her cheek as she met his gaze. "You said that you trust me. Did you say an untruth?" She shook her head, unable to speak. "This is who I am, Sweet Rune, and I like this. I need to be in control. Will you give me this one request? Allow me to give you what you need. Can you do that?"

She took a deep breath. Rune knew deep in her heart that Rorik would never hurt her. Intentionally or otherwise. "No untruth. I trust you, Rorik. I'm just scared of what you'll do," Rune replied.

"Good girl," Rorik praised her. Rune arched her back, trying to get closer. Rorik kissed her neck before moving down to her beautiful breasts. Rune gasped as he suckled on one breast, lashing at the nipple with his tongue while pinching the nipple with his thumb and forefinger.

Rorik released the breast with a pop and proudly gazed at his results. Both hardened little nubs were red from hid ministrations, and Rune panted wildly as she waited for his next assault. "To alleviate your fears, my sweet Rune, I will tell you everything I will be doing to you." Rorik sent her a wicked grin. "Since you so graciously allowed me to release first, you will have no less than three releases before we start the ritual. First, you will come on my tongue and then on my fingers," he paused to tweak her nipples again to keep them taunt.

"That's only twice," Rune panted.

Rorik chuckled in response. "The third might be a shock to you, I think." He sucked and nibbled on one nipple while his fingers molded and pinched the other. Rune wriggled at the assault. She craved more.

Rorik growled as he sucked a nipple deep into his mouth, his tongue teasingly swirled around the areola. His gentle nips sent an ache straight to her core.

Rune struggled against the bindings, but the silk held firm. Wetness soaked her thighs at the excitement. Rorik could do anything he wished to her, anything.

Rorik's mouth and fingers switched sides. He sucked until both nipples were a deeper color. "Perfect," he reverently whispered as he admired his work.

Slowly, he moved lower. He left a wet trail down Rune's abdomen as he swirled his tongue around her belly button. He smiled against her belly at Rune's breathless giggle before moving even lower to the wet ebony curls protecting her mound. He pushed her legs apart, settled between them, and inhaled her perfect musk scent. "I can't wait to bury myself in you again. To slide into your slick wet pussy, to recite the Mating Pledge and make you mine for all time."

Rorik focused on her sex. He stared for so long that Rune blushed from the exposure. Rorik nuzzled her mound as he looked into her eyes. "Suddenly bashful, Little One?"

He smiled wickedly. “We can’t have that, now, can we?” Rorik retrieved two more silk bindings and quickly encircled her ankles before attaching them to the bed posts. When finished, Rune laid wide open to his scrutiny.

“This is what I want. Your delectable, sweet pussy is open and waiting for me to do with as I please. Anything I please.” Rorik traced her slit with his finger and spread the moisture from her clit to her ass. Rune jerked with a cry at the unfamiliar touch at her back hole. “I will have you here as well, my Sweet Rune. I want to feel your tight hole grip my cock so hard while you squirm underneath me. Begging me for your release.”

Rune jerked at the rush of sensations that coursed through her body. It's only a slight jerk, however. Her current position left her helpless before him. She couldn’t believe his words. Did he want to touch her there? The night before, his cock had filled her pussy to the point of pain. It couldn’t possibly fit there, could it? Rune shook her head in denial. “It won’t fit,” she voiced her concern.

Rorik chuckled as his fingers continued their path between clit and ass. “On the contrary, Little One, I think I will fit perfectly. We have to make you ready for me, that’s all.” He swirled more moisture around her ass before returning to her cunt and shoving a finger inside her tight pussy. His mouth found hers, and his tongue danced with Rune’s as his finger slowly fucked her vulva.

After a few strokes, a second finger pushed in deeper. Rune writhed under Rorik’s ministrations. She tore away from his mouth with a cry. "Please." She needed him to move harder.

"Please, what, my sweet Rune? What do you need? Tell your mate what you need, and you shall have it."

"Please. More. Harder." Rune gasped each word as Rorik's fingers moved deep within her sheath.

"And harder you shall have." Instantly, his fingers dove into her, over and over. He added a third finger that found a sensitive spot and had Rune shrieking in ecstasy within moments.

As the last spasm faded, Rune's brain decided it could function again, and she opened her eyes to Rorik's beautiful smile. "Little One, that was the first. Now you are ready for the next one." He shifted his position between her legs and traced his cock along her soaking wet folds. Her cream coated his shaft as he teased them both with his actions.

From her vantage point, Rorik was huge. Too big to fit inside her, though she knew he had before. Fear had Rune struggling against her bindings again as his length settled against her pussy. He drove into her in one slow, determined thrust. The ache was intense, and she struggled to escape his invasion.

Rorik went as deep as he could, pressing his groin to hers. Her channel was tight around his shaft, holding him in the most pleasurable grip he could ask for. He controlled himself, keeping as still as possible to allow Rune time to adapt to his size. He watched his mate's face turn from pinched discomfort to warm delight.

He leaned in to kiss her before moving to her breasts. He caressed and nuzzled them before taking one swollen nipple into his mouth. He alternated between breasts, suckling one while lightly pinching the other. Rune grew wetter at his ministrations.

Once he deemed her ready, Rorik slowly slid in and out of her slick heat. He groaned as he fucked his mate. He powered into her hot body slowly and steadily and then retreated. Rune whimpered and thrashed at his slow pace, begging for him to move faster.

"Not yet, my love. This one, we do my way." He continued with his pace, and his hands moved to her hips. "Your channel is so slick and hot. I love the way it grips my cock so tight. I love your body. I could get lost in its softness. I can see your beautiful skin tremble under my hands." Rorik felt her muscles tighten under him, and he stopped his thrusts. Rune quailed at being denied release. He started again once she had calmed, repeating the process a few more times before Rune begged for mercy.

"Soon, my sweet Rune," he whispered as he thrust steadily. He gathered her cream with his fingers, swirled around her tight back hole, and slowly pressed in. Rune cried out at the foreign intrusion. Her legs jerked, fighting the bindings holding her open. "Relax, my sweet. Let me in," he murmured as his finger entered her reluctant hole. His finger matched his thrusts as he watched Rune, and her trembling grew stronger. She shrieked and groaned as her eyes glazed over.

"Rorik!" Rune shouted. The orgasm caught her off guard with its intensity as she hurled into oblivion for a second time. Rorik squeezed the base of his cock to avoid following his mate. He stayed still, watching her face in ecstasy. He saw the beautiful, passionate woman the Old Gods had sent to him, and he vowed to protect her with his life.

Rune opened her eyes moments later. "That was two, my sweetness." Rorik smiled lovingly at his mate. "Now, I will prepare you for the last." Rune whimpered. She was already boneless from the last two orgasms and didn't know how to survive the next.

Rorik moved around the bed out of Rune's sight. "Rorik?" she called out, suddenly nervous. She heard a drawer open and then shut.

"Relax, my Sweet Rune. I'm here." Rorik appeared by her side. "I needed to get something to help you during this next part." Rorik showed her the small bottle he held in his hand. "How are your hands and shoulders? Are they sore? Do we need to stop?"

Rune moved her arms. She was still secured, but the restraints weren't tight. "I'm okay, Sir."

"Good. Let's continue." Rorik opened the bottle and poured its contents on his fingers. "This will be a little cool, but it should warm up quickly," he said. Rune felt the coolness around her rosette and jerked away even though he had warned her. The restraints wouldn't let her move far, but she heard Rorik hum in approval. "That's right, my sweet Rune, push against my finger," he murmured repeatedly.

One digit eased into her back channel. Rune kicked out her legs at the uncomfortable intrusion. "Rorik!" Rune gasped. After the initial shock, the oil warmed her back hole, and Rune groaned as the feeling turned painful to pleasurable. Rune whimpered as Rorik pressed a second finger into her channel.

"People use this oil to relax the body's muscles, and it also has a numbing compound found only here on Dradus Prime. It should help ease any pain or discomfort you may have this first time." Rorik explained as he added a third digit, scissoring his fingers to stretch out her entrance. "I can hardly wait to get inside this tight sheath. I have a feeling you'll fit me like a glove. I'll have to be careful not to lose control."

"Please, Rorik," Rune whispered, fighting the bondage. She needed him inside her immediately, or she would go insane.

"What do you need, sweet Rune? Tell me, and you shall have it."

"You, inside me, now. Please, Sir," Rune almost screamed the last word as Rorik violently plunged his fingers into her back hole.

"I'm already inside of you," he teased Rune. "What more could you want?" He asked, flexing his fingers inside her body. "Tell me exactly what you need."

"Please, Sir," Rune gasped, blushing bright red as she made her request. "I need your cock in my ass now, Sir."

"That's what I was waiting for. Request granted. I think I've teased both of us too much already." Rune whimpered at the loss of his fingers, but seconds later, something much bigger pressed into her hole. "Take a deep breath, Sweet Rune, and push out against me. That's it. Good girl." Rorik quickly untied her ankles and pressed them against her until her knees hit her chest. The oil, along with the change of angle, made him slip easily inside.

Rune felt Rorik's cock press forward, slowly thrusting into and retreating. A groan rumbled in his chest that vibrated through her. "So tight. Feels so good."

"Harder," Rune groaned as he bottomed out in her ass.

"Yes," he replied but immediately withdrew from her body. Rune cried out with dismay before her world flipped over, and she was on her stomach. Roughly, Rorik shoved her head into the mattress and lifted her ass before plowing back into her body. His bruising fingers held her hips as he rammed into her channel repeatedly.

Rune screamed into the bedding, unable to do anything but take his brutal loving, and she loved every minute of this fucking. Flesh slapped against flesh. Rune's breasts jiggled as Rorik viciously thrust into her channel. His actions were raw and untamed as his grunts joined her cries and sweat coated their skin. The scent of sex filled the room. Rune could feel the beginnings of her climax. Rorik leaned over her back, and one hand moved to her clit. "Come for me, my sweet," he commanded, pinched her nub. Her body followed his rough command and detonated, sending her into orbit.

Rorik quickly gripped the base of his cock to avoid his release. He was hurting, but they would be true mates the next time he was released. He held on as Rune's body quaked. Tremors shook her body as the aftershocks of her release coursed through her delectable body.

"That was number three," Rorik said. His arms slid around her torso and held her tight. He chuckled at her soft whimper. Sounds of ragged breathing filled the room.

"You're going to kill me," she grumbled when she found her breath and her heartbeat calmed.

Rorik turned Rune over and found his place at her core. "I'll be just a moment, my sweet," Rorik kissed her forehead and entered the cleansing room. She heard the water running but couldn't move from her position. Rorik was back a minute later with a warm cloth. Rune blushed as he wiped the oil away from her backside. Once satisfied, he tossed the material to the side and positioned himself again at her mound.

"Now we start the ritual." He smiled at the sated look on his mate's face. "Don't worry. It won't be long now. I don't think I can last much longer." Rorik slid into her warm, wet sheath, and it felt like he was home. Never before had a joining touched him like this. He drew back slowly and thrust to the hilt. He slowly rocks into her with small thrusts. "You are mine to protect, love, honor, and cherish." Electricity swirled in the air around them at his first words.

"I give you my undying love."

"I give you all that I am and all that I will be."

"You are mine to treasure, and until death takes me from your side, I am yours'"

"Before the Old Gods, I proclaim you as my mate." Rorik rocked forward and kissed her passionately on her lips. "Now you need to say the words back to me, my sweet," he nuzzled her neck as he started his rocking thrusts again.

"You are mine to protect, love, honor, and cherish."

"I give you my undying love."

"I give you all that I am and all that I will be."

"You are mine to treasure, and until death takes me from your side, I am yours."

"Before the Old Gods, I proclaim you as my mate." At her final words, Rorik gripped Rune in a tight embrace and thrust, bottoming out at her cervix. He continued to pound into her warmth until she felt her core turn to lava. Rune wrapped her arms around him and screamed as Rorik earnestly continued his thrusting.

"Rorik!" she screamed, and he roared as they came together as one. Rune felt a burning sensation on her chest, over her heart, but she didn't care as the pain turned to bliss almost immediately.

Rorik carefully rolled to the side. He didn't want to crush his mate with his weight. They both lay panting, trying to recover. Once he could move again, Rorik pulled her to him and positioned her boneless body where he wanted her. "Sleep, my sweet. Tomorrow is a new day." Her breaths evened out moments later, and he watched his mate sleep.

Rorik gathered the blankets and covered them both. He fell asleep with his mate on his chest and a smile on his face.

Rune woke up to Bane licking her face. Groaning, she hid her face under the blankets only to have a cold nose tickle her ear. "Ours! Happy! Happy! You are ours now, forever!" his excited thoughts made her smile. A chuckle from her back let her know Bane was also projecting his excitement to Rorik. "Tempest gone now! Go now!" his excited thoughts continued as he nudged Rune with his nose.

"Is the snowstorm over?" she asked. She burrowed deeper under the covers. Rorik had given her more orgasms than she could count last night.

Rorik shuffled out of bed to the window. "Looks like Bane is right. The tempest is over." He crawled back into bed. "We have one last thing to do. After that, we can leave whenever you're ready. Then we can take you home."

"What one last thing? I thought this was home," she said.

"No, this place is my mountain retreat. Since the accident, I've spent more time here than at my other dwelling, but my home is in the city. The last thing I must do for you, my sweet, is what I promised you last night." Rorik chuckled and kissed her nose at her confused look. "Offspring."

He watched as his mate's face transformed. Happiness, joy, and a mischievous look crossed her face in seconds. "Really? Please don't tease me."

Rorik wrapped Rune in his arms. "Nothing would bring me more pleasure than to watch your belly grow round with my offspring."

"What do we do?" Rune asked breathlessly. Her sore parts were now aching with need.

"On the mat, hands and knees, facing away," Rorik growled. Rune scrambled to comply. Rorik proved last night that she would never be left wanting if she obeyed his commands.

Rorik watched his mate follow what he asked. He thanked the Old Gods again for giving him someone to treasure for the rest of his life. "Spread your knees out a little more. That's it, good girl. Lower your head to the mat, and lift your hips. Yes. Right there," Rorik guided Rune to where he wanted her body. "Your pretty pink lips are waiting for me, aren't they," he murmured, his finger sliding across her dew. "You're already wet."

"Only for you, Rorik. Only for you," Rune moaned as his fingers played with her netherlips. His hard cock stood out straight. Pointing to where it wanted to be. Rorik fisted his shaft, moving from root to tip and back. He positioned himself between her legs.

"The Old Gods have blessed our union. If they are willing, they will also bless us with offspring."

"I want as many as you will give me, my mate," Rune replied as Rorik pressed the head of his cock against Rune's pussy. Her lips were a pretty pink, and moisture coated her thighs.

"Are you ready for me, my sweet?"

"You know I am. I'll never get enough of you."

Hands-on her hips, Rorik pushed inside her wet, inviting warmth, thrusting in at once. Both groaned in unison at the feel of him fully seated inside Rune. He growled when Rune pushed back against him, shoving him further inside. He couldn't wait to show her his mark on her. It was directly over her heart. At first, he was confused this morning when he couldn't find the spot on her right side. Then he remembered her telling him that a human heart was on the left side of the body. Her mark was also on him; he knew she would love it.

"Rorik," Rune groaned in frustration. "Just do it." Rune wasn't a patient person, and the waiting was almost unbearable.

"Whatever my mate wants," Rorik replied before withdrawing and shoving back into her waiting heat. "Go slow," he thought. "Want to make this last,"

Rorik started slow, his thrusts increasing in speed with each inward thrust. "Rorik, I love you," Rune cried, breaking his restraint. The sleeping mat rocked with each hard thrust as he began to fuck his mate. Rune's sighs and groans made his cock swell with his impending release.

He reached around her and found her clit, tweaking the sensitive nub with the right amount of pressure. "Come."

Rune's body tightened, and her pussy spasmed around him as she exploded at his command. Rorik's release shot through the tip of his cock and flooded her womb with his seed. He continued to pound into her until they both lay spent on the mat.

"Wait, I can't leave," she said while Rorik packed and Bane bounded around. "I have nothing to wear outside. Your shirts are fine here, but what will I wear?"

Rorik chuckled and tickled her sides until she squealed with laughter. His heart was lighter than it had felt in years. It made him feel good to give his mate whatever she needed. "My coverings will work until we get into the city. We will stop at a female coverings shop so you can pick out anything your heart desires."

Rune smiled at her mate, her chest still heaving from the tickling. "You are a fearless male to go clothes shopping with a woman," she giggled at his worried look. "Don't worry. I'll make it fun for you, too. Ever heard of a fashion show?" His negative response made her laugh even more. "Prepare yourself, my love. You're in for a real treat."

A few hours later, Rorik had her dressed in his smallest coverings, even though they still hung off her tiny body. Bundled up to stop the chill, she was in the front seat of his land speeder. Bane happily jumped into the back with the leftover food stores.

Before he got in to leave, Rorik looked back at the cabin with fear. It had been so long since he had moved here. He started sweating, his hands shaking uncontrollably, and he fought to breathe. He couldn't do this. He needed to stay where it was safe. He couldn't face those people, their looks of disgust and fear.

A hand slapped his chest, sending those faces back into his memory. “You’re okay, Rorik. I’m here now. I need you to help me.” He looked down into the concerned face of his beautiful mate. “Just look at me, my love,” she waited until his eyes focused on hers. “You are mine to protect, love, honor, and cherish. I give you my undying love. I give you all that I am and all that I will be. You are mine to treasure, and until death takes me from your side, I am yours. Before the Old Gods, I proclaim you as my mate,” she again recited the bonding words she had spoken last night. “I love you. I won’t let anything happen to you.”

Rorik could feel the panic receding, thanks to Rune. He hated feeling weak, as if he didn’t have control over his body. Her eyes didn’t show the pity he thought would be there. Instead, he only saw love and concern. He gave her a trembling smile. “Thank you,” he whispered.

Rune smiled and pulled him down for a passionate kiss. “I’ll do anything for you,” she said, trying to catch her breath. “Now, let’s go,” she patted his chest. “I need my coverings and want to see your home.”

Rorik gently kissed her hand. “Your wish is my command.”

It was dark again when he pulled into his garage. He parked as quickly as he could. It was frigid outside, and he needed to get his mate inside their home before she froze. At their house, he still couldn’t believe that the Old Gods had deemed him worthy of a mate. He shook Rune, trying to wake her up. She had fallen asleep after their shopping spree in town. She stirred but didn’t open her eyes.

Rorik gently carried her upstairs to their sleeping mat while Bane checked the perimeter. The Wolf-Beast was more diligent now that he had Rune to protect. After Rorik brought in all her purchases, Rorik realized she hadn't moved a muscle. She was still in the same position where he had left her. After making sure Bane had settled for the night, he carefully removed her coverings, then his own, before sliding in beside her for the night.

Chapter Seven

Rune stood in the greeting room of his parent's home. She didn't know what to expect, but this home bordered on being a palace. The place was as massive as it was extravagant. Everywhere she looked, she saw opulence, verging on pretentious.

"Rorik, my love! It's about time you came home!" The voice came from a beautiful woman who looked to be in her late fifties. She was dressed immaculately in a long flowing dress, and her hair looked perfect in a tight bun. She stopped when she spied Rune. "And who is this, Rorik?"

"Majka, I would like to introduce you to my mate, Rune." Rorik pulled her close to him. He kissed her temple.

"Pleased to meet you," she said hesitantly.

The woman stared down at Rune. Her elevator eyes took in everything from her hair to her pale green dress, right down to her matching shoes. Rune had been nervous about meeting his mother, his Majka. She reminded herself. She needed to start learning the language and not rely on her translator. She chose her outfit for Rorik. Pale green, the color of her eyes, was his favorite color.

"You're not good enough for my son," she said bluntly. She continued speaking to Rorik, ignoring her completely. "Where ever did you find this pathetic creature? I know you desperately want to find your mate, but grabbing riffraff off the street is not the way. I know with your looks now, your mate will have issues. She will have to look past, but…."

"That's enough! Stop being a bitch!" Rune said through clenched teeth. First, this woman insulted her that she could live. She was, after all, a stranger on this planet. But to humiliate her son, even unintentionally, Rune could not stay silent. "How dare you insult your son!" She stepped forward, her finger close to the woman's chest. "Rorik is the sexiest male I have ever seen. How dare you insinuate that he is any less because of his scars! Scars he received by saving the men in your mines. He is a hero and should be treated as such!"

"Shh, Sweet Rune. He pulled his mate back into his arms. His chest was full of pride for defending him, even for his family. He knew his Majka didn't mean to talk down to him. She didn't mean it the way that came out," Rorik said.

Rune turned in his arms and clasped her hands behind his back. She looked into his eyes. "You forget, you are mine to protect, love, honor, and cherish, and I will protect you, no matter the source. Even if it's your family."

"You're mated?" his majka shrieked. Rune could see the disgust in her eyes. "I don't see any mark." She grabbed at Rune's dress to check her collarbone.

"Majka, enough!" Rorik growled, pulling Rune to him, annoyed by her actions. "Yes, we are mated," he punctuated each word. Anger vibrated off his body. He never realized how insensitive his Majka was. He saw how she looked at his mate, and he didn't like it. "No, we don't have to prove it to you or anyone else."

"Be happy for our boy, Irka. You've been worried about him since the accident," an older male said as he entered the room. “Make our new daughter welcome.” He looked to Rune. “Welcome to our family, young one. You may call me Calwin or, if you wish, Patri. I’m sorry, but I didn’t catch your name.”

Rune looked at an older version of Rorik. Tall, broad shoulders and long hair, though streaked with grey, gave him an aura of power, much like Rorik. This male was accustomed to being in charge. “Thank you. You have a lovely home. My name is Rune, and it’s a pleasure to meet you.”

“Patri, when did you get home? I wasn’t expecting you until our last meal,” Rorik said, shaking his father’s hand in welcome.

“I’ve started working less since the accident,” Rorik’s Patri replied. “I’ve allowed your bruder, Daewon, to take over most of the business.” He looked hesitant for a moment. “How long will you be staying in the city? Your bruder and I must discuss a few things while you’re here.”

“Rune is new to this planet, and I want to show her everything. We also need to contact her Majka. Do you know anyone who can get a call to the Alliance? Slavers destroyed her ship, and her majka doesn’t know that her daughter lives.”

“I suppose you would want your Majka to be present at the mating celebration?” Irka said with a sneer.

Rune smiled sweetly. Arguing with her mother-in-law was counter-productive at this point. “Yes, Irka. That was the plan. After all, I might have conceived already, and I want my mom with me every step of the way," she replied, rubbing her belly. She watched with silent glee as Irka turned red at using her given name.

"I know just who to comm," Calwin replied. "I know a male who does business with a few people on Earth." He stopped and looked at Rune. "It will take up to sixty cycles one way, my dear. It is not a short trip," he warned. "Let me com my friend first; see if he has any ships close. That would make the wait less for both parties." He quickly walked off to an adjacent room.

"Where is Bane, darling?" Irka asked her son, trying to change the subject.

Rorik chuckled. "He took off into the surrounding woods. With the Thaw almost here, he was eager to have a female's company. I don't think we'll see him for a few cycles."

"I have good news, my dear," Calwin announced to Rune as he strode out of his office. "My friend has a ship heading to Earth as we speak. He will wait for my call and bring your Majka back. If all goes well, you should see her in person soon. Now come with me. I have a representative from the Alliance on hold. He is desperate to see you, my dear."

A thin, harried-looking man stood in front of the monitor. "Ms. Shadow! It's so good to see you! Is there anyone else with you? From the ship?" he asked, hope etched across his face.

"Hello there. No, I'm the only one I know who landed here on Dradus Prime. Well, crashed is more like it, but the snow cushioned my landing."

The man's face fell at the news. "You are the first one to contact us, Ms. Shadow. I'm afraid you are the sole survivor."

Tears filled Rune's eyes, threatening to spill over. "I would like to get a message to my mother, please," she answered. She refused to think about the other women at the moment. "Tell me, how long have I been missing?"

The man paled. "It has been four months since you left Earth. Everyone has been presumed dead." He took a deep breath and smiled into the monitor. "Your mother is on her way here now, Ms. Shadow. We notified her as soon as Mr. StoneBlade called. She should be here shortly. Please wait."

Rune's deep, shaky breath brought Rorik to her side. He said nothing but wrapped her in his embrace and kissed her temple. Rune didn't need comments. Rorik knew what she needed at that moment and gave it to her. She was safe in his arms.

They stood there for quite a while until the thin man returned to the monitor. "Ms. Shadow? Are you still there?"

"Yes, I'm here," she replied. Her voice was barely above a whisper.

The man nodded, then motioned off-screen for someone to come forward. "What is going on?" Abigail asked the man. Her back was toward the monitor. The man just smiled and turned her around.

"Rune?" she asked. Her face was paler than usual. Her bloodshot eyes welled with tears. "Oh. My. God! Rune, is that you? My baby girl! You came back to me!" she wailed with excitement. Tears streaked down her cheeks.

Rune cut into her almost hysterical babbling. "Mom, Mom, MOM!" Abigail stopped her chattering. "I'm fine, Mom. I'm sorry I didn't call sooner. The planet I landed on was in the middle of a snowstorm. We just got into the city. I called as soon as I could."

"We?" Abigail asked, drying her eyes. Her deep breaths were stuttering as she gazed at her daughter.

Rune shook her head. Trust her mom to pick on just that one word from her single daughter. "Yes, Mom. We. I want you to meet someone." She dragged Rorik by the wrist in front of the monitor. "Mom, I want you to meet Rorik, my mate," she said. Her eyes loving beamed at him.

"Pleased to meet you, ma'am," Rorik said. He returned Rune's smile.

Abigail's eyes widened at the scarred face of the man standing beside her daughter. She looked between the two and sighed. She wouldn't say it, but that was what she wanted. Someone to gaze at her as this massive male looked at her daughter. "Well, now, they sure grow 'em big on that planet, don't they?" she said, staring at Rorik.

"Mother!" Rune exclaimed.

Abigail noticed the wide eyes and scandalous look on her daughter. Realizing what she had said, she blushed as well. "I didn't mean that! Honestly," she huffed. "That is too much information, young lady." She said as she tried to keep a straight face amid Rune's giggling. The giggling increased at Rorik's confused look. Abigail decided to get back on topic. "Young man," she started. Her eyes narrowed in concern at Rorik. "Do you love my daughter? Will you give her everything she desires?"

Rorik's smile transformed his face, and Abigail saw the love for her Rune in his eyes. "I do, and I will, ma'am. I will love my sweet Rune until I no longer walk this planet."

"Awe," Rune teared up. Before she did what she wanted and attacked her mate where they stood, she looked at Abigail. "Mom, we're already mated, but his family is having a mating ceremony and celebration for us. I want you to be here for that and for…." Rune bit her lip. With a deep breath, she added, "And for the pregnancy."

"You're having a baby!" she shrieked. She couldn't believe it. Her baby was going to have a baby.

"We don't know just yet, but if I'm not now, then I will be soon," she replied with blushing cheeks.

"Well, of course, I will be there. I don't know how I will get there, but I will. Where exactly are you?" Abigail rambled. Her mind was on what she needed to do before she left.

"I'm on a planet called Dradus Prime. It's not in the Alliance, so Rorik's patri, dad, is working on getting a ship to pick you up." Rorik kissed Rune's temple and left her to finish speaking with her mom. "My Patri has arranged your travel, ma'am," he addressed Abigail. "My Patri's friend has a ship near Earth. It can be there in three cycles of time. Is that enough time to prepare for your journey?"

"Yes, that should be enough time. Call me Abigail or Mom. Ma'am makes me feel old," tears welled in her eyes. "I can't believe I'll soon be able to hug my baby again." Her voice was breaking as the tears fell.

"Ma'am, er Abigail, the ship will meet you at the Alliance headquarters in three cycles. Patri has instructed the Alliance to provide a translator for your trip. It will take approximately sixty cycles to Dradus Prime. We will meet you when you arrive," he said, quickly kissing Rune and leaving again. Female tears made him uneasy. They would cry if they were happy or sad, and he could never figure out which to solve their troubles.

"I think we made him nervous," Rune laughed through her tears. She was a sympathy crier. If her mother cried, then so did she. She ended the call several minutes later and left to find Rorik.

Smiling, she wiped her tears as she returned to the greeting room. Not looking, she ran into a rigid body. "Oh, I'm so sorry! I didn't mean to…" Her words faded as she looked up into angry eyes.

"You must be the trash Majka said has her dirty claws in my little bruder," he snarled. "You will leave our home at once and never return. Forget about Rorik. He won't give you any more credits."

Rune realized that Irka had called in reinforcements to get rid of her. Eyes narrowed, she glared at the male. He looked like Rorik and Calwin. He had called Rorik 'little bruder,' so this was Daewon. "First off, I'm not trash or what your majka called riffraff. I crashed onto this planet, and Rorik saved my life. We fell in love and are now mated. If your sweet majka can't handle that fact, then we will have nothing to do with her or anyone else," she growled at him and poked him in the chest.

"What's going on? Rune, are you all right? I felt your anger." Rorik came up behind her and pulled her to his chest. "Daewon, what are you doing here?"

Rune answered for him. "Your bruder here was in the process of trying to throw me out. He thinks I have my dirty claws in you for your money and wants to get rid of me," she glared at the male, daring him to contradict her.

"What? How did you get that idea? I haven't even introduced you two yet," Rorik looked between his mate and his bruder, concerned by his bruder's actions. His family had never behaved this way before.

"That's what your Majka told him," Rune answered for his bruder again.

"What's going on here?" Calwin asked. He walked up beside Rorik. "Daewon, good to see you. What are you doing here?"

"I called him," Irka announced. She stood next to her oldest. "She," pointed at Rune, "doesn't belong here. I will not have an unvetted female in the family. This family is too important to allow just anyone to mate into."

"Majka!" Rorik exclaimed. He would never have believed it if he hadn't heard it himself. His majka was acting like an entitled bitch. He never knew that she thought their family was above everyone else's.

"Wow, conceited much?" Rune replied sassily. "Let me guess, you vetted Solaini and approved of her. She was the gold digger, not me. I don't care about all your credits. I would be just as happy in the cabin in the mountains. All I need is Rorik and Bane to be happy. Know why? Because they make me happy, not the credits."

Suddenly, Bane bolted through the door, snarling at the family. He stopped in front of Rune and Rorik, protecting them. The fur on his back raised, and he growled at Irka and Daewon. Saliva dripped down its snarling canines. Protect ours, his thoughts projected to everyone.

"Awe, good boy," Rune said, scratching his ears. She leaned down slightly and kissed his snout. Everyone stared in awe at Rune, unafraid of Bane's display of protectiveness. Even Rorik had never seen Bane display this level of possessiveness. "Who's a sweet boy?" Rune crooned at Bane.

Bane growled again, showing his teeth, before succumbing to Rune's words and sitting down. He whined once and licked her face, tail swishing on the floor. Ours. Forever. Protect. Bane replied.

Calwin chuckled, breaking the stunned silence in the room. "Well, there you have it, Irka. Bane has claimed her. Remember, he hated Solaini on sight. Our boy chose better than we did."

"My apologies, Rune. I should never have assumed. Please forgive me," Daewon said as he bowed low as a sign of respect. His parents had chosen his mate as was their custom, but his wolf beast had never come to his mate's defense as Bane had just done.

Rune looked into Rorik's loving eyes, smiling at his slight nod. She faced Daewon. "Apology accepted. I hope we can be friends." He grinned with her and saw her love for his bruder in her eyes. Scars and all, she adored his baby bruder. His chest tightened with the reminder of the accident. However, his investigations revealed that it had not been an accident. Someone had sabotaged the work site, and he needed to talk to Rorik about it.

Chapter Eight

Abigail couldn't believe that she was leaving Earth on a spaceship. Her daughter was braver than ever, going off into the unknown as she did. She was shaking in her shoes, waiting in the lobby of the Alliance Headquarters.

"Ms. Shadow?" a woman wearing a lab coat approached her. Abigail could only nod. "My name is Doctor Emma Taylor. Please follow me, and I will implant your translator before your ship arrives."

"Is this the same translator you gave my daughter?"

"Yes, ma'am," Doctor Taylor nodded. "All Interstellar Brides have it installed, though it usually is done on the way to the first planet."

Abigail sat in a lounge that looked like it was for VIPs or the rich and famous. Everything she could want was there at no charge to her. The doors to the room slid open, and in walked the most beautiful male specimen she had ever seen. Abigail sipped water when she desperately wanted an alcoholic beverage to calm her nerves.

Kilam Stormfury strode into the room as if he owned it. He would if it were not for the laws governing the small planet. He possessed the largest and most profitable import/export business on Dradius Prime. He towered over the males in the building at six feet four inches. He knew some Earthers were as tall as he was, but he had yet to meet one.

He surveyed the room, looking for the female his best friend had asked him to retrieve for his son's mating ceremony. His breath caught in his chest as he spied on the only female in the room. Her shoulder-length black hair looked like the spun silk he bought from Earth merchants, and her eyes the color of the smaras his friend mined on Dradius Prime. He stared at her exotic body, and his body responded. He suddenly realized he had gazed for too long, and this beautiful female looked nervous. "Abigail? Abigail Shadow?" he asked, his voice cracking embarrassingly.

He waited for her to nod before he continued. "My name is Kilam of the Clan Stonefury," he said with a bow. "It is my pleasure to escort you to Dradius Prime for your daughter's mating ceremony."

Abigail blushed profusely. How in the world would she survive for two months with this man? She closely watched as he walked toward her and her luggage. He was about a foot taller than her, five feet 4-inch height. Sunlight caressed his light brown hair, detailing the various colors within the strands. His eyes reminded Abigail of the waters of the Caribbean beach she had visited before she had Rune.

"Let me get this for you," he said, reaching for her suitcase.

"Thank you, Kilam," she replied. "I didn't know what to bring, so I threw a few things together."

Kilam grunted as he handled the case. "Most females I know would have brought everything they owned," he commented gruffly.

"Oh, no!" Abigail looked horrified at the thought. "I don't know how long I can stay. I didn't want to be presumptuous like that. If I need something, I can find a way to get it. I have money, so I'd only need a way to convert it to your currency," Abigail stated.

Kilam stood, shocked for a moment. He had never met a female who didn't demand someone pay for their desires. This woman was one in a million indeed. "Welcome to the Fury," he said, sweepingly at his spacecraft.

Time had flown by, and now Rune was waiting for the Fury to land. She had spoken to her mom on vidscreen just before she departed from Earth almost two months ago. Rune couldn't wait to tell her about the ceremony, which would take place in two cycles, and talk about her trip. She thought she also had news on another subject, smiling as she rubbed her belly. She couldn't thank Calwin's friend enough for diverting his ship to pick up her mother and bring her to Dradus Prime.

Rorik wrapped his arms around her waist from behind. He kissed her temple and nuzzled her neck. "How are you feeling, my sweet Rune? Is the baby causing you trouble?"

Rune giggled at her mate. "No, I'm feeling fine. I can't wait to see my mom again after so long." They stood in the transfer station above Dradius Prime, waiting for the Fury to dock. Rune was as excited as a child on Christmas morning. The Thaw, as the citizens of Dradius Prime called what people on Earth called Spring, was in full bloom. Plants and flowers she had never seen the like of before bloomed across the planet. Rune wore the same dress when she met Irka and Calwin all those days ago.

Finally, the ship docked safely, and the ramp lowered. The first person she saw wasn't her mother but a large, handsome male. He descended the ramp and clasped Rorick on the back. "Good to see you, Rorik!" he exclaimed.

Rorik smiled and shook his hand. "This is my mate, Rune," he said, kissing her hair. "Rune, may I introduce you to a great family friend, Kilam of the Clan Stormfury."

Rune smiled and shook his hand, angling her body to look around him. "Pleased to meet you, Mr. Stormfury. May I ask where my mother is?"

Kilam looked at his friend's mate. "You're just as beautiful as your mother," he replied without thought.

Rune raised an eyebrow at Kilam. "Is that so," she smirked. "I see. So that's how it is. Mom and I have many things to discuss, it seems." Rune heard hurried footsteps and turned to see her mom running toward her. Rune squealed in excitement and rushed to meet her halfway. They collided in a mass of hugs and tears, both women talking simultaneously.

"Mom! You look great! I'm so happy to see you!" Rune said between her tears of joy.

"My baby! I've missed you so much!" Abigail cried in her daughter's arms.

The women talked so fast that neither Rorik nor Kilam could understand them. The two men watched their women hugging and crying for a few minutes. "We should probably move them to the transport," Kilam said, his eyes never leaving Abigail.

"Agreed," Rorik replied, his gaze never leaving his mate.

"Where is your transport?" Kilam asked, slowly approaching the women as if they were wild Zercats ready to attack.

"It's just around the corner," Rorik said, carefully putting a hand on Rune.

"No!" the women shouted in unison, their arms tightening around each other. "I won't lose my baby again!"

"You won't lose her, kaeri, my promise," Kilam said quietly.

"Nor will she, my sweet," Rorik also promised, running a soft hand across her cheek and kissing her forehead. "Let's go back to the house to be comfortable talking and get caught up on the last few months."

That's a good idea," Rune softly said as she watched her mom and the giant man.

The day had finally arrived—the day of her Mating Ceremony. Rorik discussed the details of the ceremony with her and her mother yesterday. Rune thought it was reminiscent of ancient Earth's marriage ceremony, and she could hardly wait. She had dreamed of this day, and it had finally come.

She stood before a long mirror, looking for anything out of place. She wore a floor-length pale green dress with dark green smaras sewn into the bodice. Stylists had carefully braided tiny white flowers into her hair. “You look beautiful,” her mother said behind her. “I can’t believe my baby is getting married,” she declared, dabbing the tears from her eyes.

“It won’t be long before you’re right where I am now, Mom. I’ve seen the way Kilam looks at you,” Rune replied, smiling and looking at her mom’s reflection in the mirror.

Abigail blushed as she straightened Rune’s dress. “It’s not like that at all.” She smiled sadly at her daughter. “He had a mate, but she died years ago.” She sighed wistfully at her daughter. “He’s not ready to let her go yet, and I won’t play second fiddle to a ghost.”

A cough from the doorway had both women turning around quickly. Rorik stood dressed in his formal attire, and Rune swooned. “You look fabulous. Do we need to do this? Let’s escape and go somewhere where we can be alone,” Rune said huskily. Her voice filled with promise.

Rorik smirked. He knew she wanted only him and loved it whenever she proclaimed it publicly. After many planetary cycles of being a recluse, he joined the world again. “After you, my sweet,” Rorik motioned for her to pass.

As the two left the room, Abigail looked into Kilam’s haunted eyes. Frowning, she glanced around before coming back to him. Abigail could tell he wanted to say something, but the words wouldn’t leave his mouth. “Is everything all right?” she asked, perplexed by his strange look.

Kilam started to shake his head but immediately nodded instead. She didn't realize it, but he had heard her words. The concept of losing Abigail because of his actions pierces his heart with terror. He had had thirty-five planetary cycles with his mate before her untimely death, and he was reluctant to find another, even just for companionship. That was until Abigail entered his life. Unfortunately, old habits are hard to break, and he realized that things would have to drastically change if he wanted Abigail to remain in his life. "It's time to take our seats," he whispered, holding his arm for her to take.

Rune proudly stood next to Rorik and waited for the music to start. Attendants had laid out a beautiful, thick red carpet at her feet. Fifteen archways dripping with colorful flowers graced the walkway that led to a raised dais. An Elder stood at the top, waiting for the happy couple to arrive.

The music started, startling Rune back into the present. Rorik smiled at her and walked with her slowly down the aisle. Bane walked in front of the couple, giving his protection and signaling to all in attendance that he approved the union.

They stood one step below the Elder as he spoke of loving each other eternally. Most of the Eldeer's words were a light hum to Rune's ears. She repeated his words when commanded, but her eyes never left Rorik's handsome face. She also heard Rorik repeat his words, and then it was time to kiss.

Rorik's lips descended onto hers in a heartbeat. His tongue was advancing, then retreating in the age-old dance. His lips were gentle as he pillaged her moist mouth.

Rune lost herself in his arms. It wasn't until the murmurs and chuckles broke through the lustful haze that she remembered where she was and that they weren't alone. Rorik finished the kiss, and the audience clapped and laughed at the flustered pair. The couple returned through the flowered archways into the receiving area.

Hours later, Rune and Rorik had changed into their reception attire to mingle with the guests. Rune smiled and nodded to everyone that wished her and Rorik well. Her face hurt. She had smiled so often.

A beautiful, tall, willowy woman approached Rune. "I don't believe you're genuinely mated," the woman said with a sneer. "I can't even see the mating mark. Mine is there for all to see," she boasted. Rune could see her mark high on her chest, close to her shoulder.

Rorik was suddenly by Rune's side. "Solaini," Rorik growled at the female. Rune watched as the woman sneered at her mate.

"Wait, you're Solaini?" Startled, the woman looked at Rune and smirked.

"Yes. I see Rorik has talked about me," she replied, looking smug at the comment.

"Oh, yes. We've discussed our pasts, and I've wanted to meet you since Rorik spoke of you," Rune replied. "I wanted to thank you from the bottom of my heart." Both Rorik and Solaini looked at Rune with surprise.

"You see," she explained with a sweet smile. "If you hadn't been such a low-life, gold-digging bitch, I never would have met my mate," Rune said gleefully. "He never would have been there to find me after my escape pod crashed. I would never have met Bane; isn't he such a sweet boy?" Rune innocently batted her eyelashes at the other woman. She knew that Bane hated Solaini.

"As I said, I wanted to thank you for being a bitch and choosing a lesser mate than my wonderful man here," Rune grabbed Rorik's hand and held it to her belly. "We're already expecting, and we couldn't be happier." Solaini looked as if she had eaten a rotten lemon. "As for our mating marks? Rorik had explained that the higher the mark, the weaker the bond. Well, you see, humans have our hearts on the left side of our bodies, opposite your kind. So when Rorik and I mated, well, we made love heart-to-heart. The Old Gods blessed our union, and as destined mates, our bond is one of the strongest." Rune looked to Rorik with a mischievous smile. "Sweetheart, could you please show your ex our mating mark? I don't think showing mine in this crowd would be appropriate."

Rorik growled at that remark. Her mating mark was too low for any male in the room to see without Rorik wanting to kill them on the spot. Without words, Rorik unbuttoned his shirt and opened it to reveal his mark directly over his heart. Rune heard the gasps from the onlookers as her words rang true. Solaini turned a bright shade of red, stomped her foot, and left the couple in the middle of the room.

"You are now my hero," another woman approached, wearing a genuine smile on her face.

Rorik relaxed and smiled back. Turning to his mate, he made the introductions. "Rune, this is my Siska, Amedea," he hugged his sister. "I'm glad you could make it."

"I wouldn't miss my baby bruder's Mating Ceremony for anything," she replied.

"Rune, Amedea is an acclaimed artist. She and her mate travel extensively to many planets," he said. Rune could hear the pride in his voice.

"A pleasure to finally meet you. Rorik has told me many stories of the three of you growing up," Rune replied, shaking the woman's hand.

Amedea groaned good-naturedly. "Remember, whatever he's told you, he's the baby of the family. It was all his fault." Her response had Rune laughing and Rorik blushing.

"Kezen! What a great party!" a tall male exclaimed, slapping Rorik on the back. Rorik smiled and returned the slap.

"Rune, my love, this cretin is my kezen, Finas. My majka and his patri are bruder and siska," he introduced the male.

Rune could see the family resemblance. Though Finas was slightly taller than Rorik, her mate had thicker muscles. The newcomer's hair and eye color were lighter than her mate's. "It's nice to meet you, Finas. I hope you're having a good time."

Finas placed his hand on his heart and gave her a deep bow. "Congratulations, you two. If there is anything you need, please don't hesitate to ask. You're family now, my new kezen." Finas winked at Rune before drifting off into the crowd.

Rorik shook his head at his kezen's antics. "I hope he finds love someday as well," he stated. He wrapped Rune up in an embrace and kissed her head.

"Why wouldn't he?" Rune asked curiously. "He seems like a nice guy."

"He is very nice, almost too nice, but that's not his problem. His problem is his wealth. He created a device that allows spaceships to create their gateway across the galaxies. The device uses our smaras to store the energy required. Because of that, his family is considerably wealthier, and the females of the planet are fighting to become family. His Majka and Patri are very cautious of any invitations they receive."

"That's such a shame. Everyone deserves to be loved for who they are, not for what they have," Rune replied sadly, looking in the direction where Finas had disappeared.

As the party was winding down and most of the guests had left, Daewon approached the happy couple. "Congratulations on a beautiful ceremony, little bruder," he said with a bow, which Rorik and Rune returned. "I apologize that I must speak of this on your special day, but it can't wait any longer."

Rorik immediately tensed at his bruder's words. Something was wrong, and he needed to protect Rune and her mother, Abigail. "What's wrong?" he asked tersely.

"It has to do with the explosions at the mine."

"That was an accident," Rorik started to say.

"That's what the officials ruled it as, but I've investigated and found evidence that it wasn't an accident." Rune inhaled quickly, and Rorik reared in shock at his bruder's words.

Chapter Nine

"The accident was two planetary cycles ago," Rorik said through clenched teeth. He couldn't believe that someone would do that. "No one came forward to take responsibility for the explosions."

"I'm sorry, bruder, to have to tell you this on your Ceremony Day, but I've received new information that your new mate's life is in danger."

Rune paled at his words. "How do they know about me? I've only been here for a few moon cycles."

Daewon smiled at his new sister-in-law. He admired her for standing up to him and his family when they first met. It had taken time for his majka to realize that her baby was indeed mated, and she could do nothing about it. "The Mating Ceremony, for one thing," he started. "Majka ensured that the ceremony was the talk of the elite social circles. She also spared no expense for my little bruder's big day. No offense to you," he bowed in respect.

"No offense taken. Irka and I have a long way to go before we're friends. That may never happen," Rune laughed. "Maybe when she gets another grandchild," she patted her slightly swollen belly. Rorik placed his hand on hers and kissed her temple.

Daewon smiled at Rune and her candor. He was slightly jealous of his little bruder. Rune looked at his bruder as if he was the center of her world, and Rorik looked at Rune the same way.

"Have Bane stay close for the night and meet me at my place tomorrow morning. I will show you everything I have then. Until then, be safe." With those final words, Daewon walked off to find his mate.

Bane, we need you, Rune silently called out. She was nervous and freaked out at the prospect that someone wanted to harm her. Within moments, Bane nudged her hand. Rune calmed slightly at his presence. "We'll leave for home immediately. I want you safe," Rorik commanded. His heart rate increased with the thought of anything happening to his mate. He knew Rune was just as distressed because she didn't argue with his command.

∞

The following day, after a restless night's sleep, they were on their way to Daewon's house across town. Bane had left early to secure the property before they got there. Rorik had done everything he could to ensure she rested, taking her countless times, but it was useless. Rune had been too apprehensive, her thoughts unwilling to let her sleep.

Rune sat stiffly beside Rorik as he piloted the transport through the streets. Her eyes looked everywhere. "We will get to the bottom of this," he said, kissing her hand as he drove. "You will be safe, my sweet Rune."

Rune smiled, complete trust in her eyes. "I know you will do your best, but you can't guarantee it unless I'm in a sealed room."

Three loud popping sounds hit the transport, shattering the windows and hitting the front compartment. Rune screamed as another transport slammed into the back end of their vehicle. Rorik hit the brakes and swerved to the left. It was no use. Between the bullet lodged into his side and the collision, his momentum forced him toward the barrier. The transport crashed to the ground with the engine hit and rolled down a steep embankment next to the travel lane. Branches snapped at the impact, jerking the vehicle down the side.

Rorik slowly came awake. His body was protesting his movements as he slowly looked at his surroundings. "Rune?" he called out, his voice cracking. "Rune?" he called with a stronger voice. He was still in the transport, his legs pinned by the crumpled wreckage. A tree branch had shattered the front shield and separated the driver's and passenger's sides, barely missing his head. He couldn't tell if his mate was there or not.

"Rune!" he yelled, his arm breaking through the leaves on the branch. His mate wasn't there, though his hand came back covered with her blood. Rorik's sight became fuzzy as darkness encroached on his vision. He tried to remain conscious, but it was no use. His last thought went to Bane. "We've been attacked. Rune is missing. Find her."

The smell of disinfectant and cleaners filled Rorik's nostrils, turning his stomach. Muffled conversations filtered into his mind as he tried to remember something. Something important. His head pounded as he attempted to open his eyes, but they were too heavy. He needed to do something, but he couldn't remember what. Darkness enveloped him as he slipped back into oblivion.

Hushed voices and a whine coaxed Rorik to rejoin the living. He forced his eyes open and immediately closed them with a groan. He turned his head and slowly opened his eyes again. Bane jumped up onto the bed and licked his companion's face. Rorik chuckled, then winced as pain exploded throughout his chest.

"Hi there," Calwin said as his mother rushed to him.

"My baby. You had us all so scared. What happened? Who did this?" Irka rattled off the questions too quickly for Rorik to comprehend.

"Rune?" he whispered his question. His family just looked at each other worriedly.

"I'm sorry, Rorik. We haven't found her yet. The accident destroyed your transport. We found a blood trail leading away from the wreckage, but it disappeared. Even Bane lost her scent," Daewon said sadly.

"Had help. Carried away," Bane growled in Rorik's head.

"I have friends in local peacekeepers. They're looking for your mate as we speak," Daewon said.

"You were going to tell us what you learned about the explosions. Tell me now," Rorik demanded.

Daewon looked at the shocked faces of his family. "I've been investigating the explosion that almost killed Rorik. Since then, our mines have had three more 'accidents.' The explosions didn't damage very much, and no one was hurt," he started.

"Why wasn't I told about this?" Calwin almost shouted, his face red with anger.

"Because I am in charge of security, and you and Majka were too worried about Rorik. I didn't want to worry you further," stated cooly.

"How long have I been here?" Rorik asked, changing the subject. He didn't think his head could handle more shouting.

"Two cycles," his Majka replied. "We are looking for Rune. I'm sorry I've been so mean to her," tears welled in her eyes. Rorik could see the regret in her eyes.

Rorik looked at his family, seeing each concern, and then at Calwin. "Patri, get me out of here."

Rune groaned, moving ever so slowly, her body screaming at every muscle twitch. Where was she? What happened? She thought, looking around at her surroundings. Her room had a dank, musty smell, like an old basement. Large stones made up the walls, and some areas were damp. The only light source was a tiny window close to the ceiling. The only furnishings in the room were the bed she woke up on and a bucket in the corner.

Rune recoiled on the bed and tried to make herself as small as possible. The door to the room swung open, and a large male approached Rune carrying a tray. The male's massive frame dwarfed the room as he placed the tray on the ground next to the mat. He stood and crossed his arms, just staring at her. His red skin reminded Rune of the Helviti race on Ferr, but this creature had four arms.

"Clak, leave us," a female voice commanded from the doorway. Clak grunted and left as ordered. Shock rushed through Rune as the female shut the door.

"Solaini? What's going on?" Rune asked. Her ribs hurt to breathe, but she composed herself. She instinctively knew that Solaini would torture her if she had the chance.

"I am in the process of getting what's mine," Solaini replied smugly. "I would have gotten it by mating Rorik, but after the explosion, I couldn't stand to look at him, let alone touch him." She shivered in disgust at the thought. "His injuries are his fault. He wasn't supposed to be there."

"What do I have to do with that?" Rune asked, though she knew what Solaini would say.

"Are you that stupid?" Solaini asked as contempt colored her words. "You're my ticket to what rightfully is mine!" she yelled, saliva dripping from her mouth. "For many planetary cycles, I've tried to get what was mine, but did they listen?" Wild, wide eyes focused on Rune. "No! They didn't! Everyone ignored me! Well, they'll never dismiss me again!" Solaini hysterically laughed, slamming the door on her way out.

Rune rose as quickly as her aching body would allow, checking the door. Sure enough, Solaini had locked it again. Dejected, Rune shuffled stale bread and a little cup of water on the tray. Rune chuckled at herself, shaking her head, and slowly ate the meal.

As she chewed, Rune thought about how she would get out of there. She could use nothing in the room as a weapon;

the tray could barely handle the bread and cup. She closed her eyes, leaned against the wall, and thought of Rorik. Was he all right? Was he hurt? Rune teared up at the thought of him hurting.

"Rorik, Bane, I love you," she whispered before falling into a restless slumber.

"Heard Rune! Will find!" Bane shouted at Rorik. Bane bounced around their home in the city.

"Bane, stop," Rorik commanded. His head was still pounding, and his body was still sore from the accident. "Everyone is out looking for Rune. We will find her," he said, his teeth clenched through the pain of thinking.

Rorik's com signaled an incoming call from Rune's frequency. "Rune, where are you, my sweet?" Rorik jerked up as he answered.

A deep, unmistakenly male voice chuckled on the other end. "The bitch lives, for now, Stoneblade," the voice replied. "If you want to see her or your unborn brat, you will do as I say," the voice continued. "We will call again tomorrow with a list of demands. Make sure you answer."

"Wait! I want proof of life!" he cried, but the caller was already gone.

The following day, Rorik sat staring at his com, silently praying for the call and his sweet Rune to be alive. "I pray to all the Old Gods. Please let my sweet Rune, as well as my child, be all right." Rorik bowed his head and repeated that phrase as a mantra. His family paced around him, eager for the call as well. Law enforcement had tapped his com so they could try to trace the origin of the ring.

"Why haven't they called yet?" Abigail cried. Kilam was immediately by her side, trying to comfort his distraught friend.

"We have to be patient. The peacekeepers will get her back."

"Daewon," Rorik called to his bruder. "Continue what you explained yesterday about these so-called accidents," he commanded. He needed to take his mind off of the impending call.

Daewon sat next to his bruder. "After your accident, the Fire Marshall investigated our security measures and determined that a faulty wire was to blame for the mishap, as he called it," Daewon sneered at the memory. "I noticed that he didn't review any security footage and did a poor job handling any collected evidence."

He took a deep breath to collect himself. "A few days after the incident, I received an offer to buy the mine. I refused, of course, but the caller demanded that I sell, stating the ongoing investigation with the Security Council about the accident."

"Now, at the time of the call, the accident investigation was not public knowledge, so I knew whoever was on the other end knew more than they should. Because of the Fire Marshall's misconduct, the Safety Council eventually fined our company for hazardous working conditions. Shortly after the verdict, I received another call demanding I sell the mine. Again, I refused. This time, the caller mentioned future issues with our other mines before ending the call."

"Why didn't you notify the Peace Keepers about any of this? Why didn't you notify me?" Calwin shouted, outraged that someone was targeting his family and his company.

"The same reason I had told you before in the hospital. Rorik was in the hospital, fighting for his life. I didn't want to worry you further about this issue as well. As for the Peace Keepers?" Daewon calmly shrugged. "I had evidence that the Fire Marshall was corrupt. Who's to say the Peacekeepers weren't as well?"

"Continue," Rorik said, rubbing his temples to ease his stress.

"Over the next two planetary cycles, three more mines had accidents: the Grimstone Mine, the Black Burrows, and the Soothill Mines. Luckily, the incident caused no major damage, and no one was injured, so I never notified the Safety Council. After each incident, though, I received either a call or a letter demanding I sell the Green Mountain Mine."

"The site of the first accident," Rorik murmured. "Why would they want that one in particular?"

At that moment, the com sounded with Rune's frequency. Everyone held their breath as Rorik answered. "I want proof of life. Let me talk to Rune," he immediately demanded.

A chuckle sounded on the other end. "Don't worry, the bitch still lives, though slightly damaged," he stated with a smile. Rorik could hear muffled voices and then silence.

"Rorik?" Rune asked a moment later.

"Rune! How are you? Do you know who did this?" he asked frantically. There was a scuffle at the other end and then more silence.

"You heard the bitch. You had your proof of life. If you want to see her alive again, sign the Green Mountain Mine to us. We will call you in two cycles to set up a meeting." The call ended before Rorik could say anything else.

"NO!" Rorik slammed down his com. Standing, he paced the room. After a few minutes, he stopped and looked at the room. Everyone had remained silent until he could collect his thoughts. "They are demanding that we sign over the Green Mountain Mine to them. They will call back in two cycles to set up the meeting."

"Is my baby all right?" Abigail quietly asked as tears flooded her eyes.

Rorik's gaze softened as he looked at his mother-in-law. "They only allowed her one word, but she sounded all right considering the circumstances." She nodded and left the room, unwilling to cry in front of others.

Rorik watched her leave before turning to his bruder. "I want to know the history of that mine, including when we purchased it and who owned it before us. Everything."

Several hours later, they had their information. Calwin immediately called his old friend. "Evam, my friend," Calwin started when the call connected. "My family and I've run into a bit of trouble, and I was hoping you could help us out." He was silent for a moment before nodding his head.

"Yes, yes. Everything is fine for the moment. Our problem is that our new daughter, Rune, has been kidnapped." Calwin again listened before putting the call on speaker.

"…spoken with the peacekeepers?" Evam asked.

"Yes, we are working closely with peacekeepers at the moment. Our issue is with the Green Mountain Mine," he stated bluntly.

"What does that mine have to do with the kidnapping?" Evam asked, confused.

"My son has informed me that we've had issues with our other mines in the past few planetary cycles. Demand for that mine follows each supposed accident."

"Wasn't an accident in that mine a few years ago that almost killed your youngest son?" Evam asked. "Why would anyone want that mine?"

"He doesn't know," Daewon commented to the group.

"I don't know what?" Evam asked, having realized he was on speaker with that remark.

"We had discovered a rich new Samra vein just before my accident. Immediately after Solaini refused me and you withdrew your allegiance, someone offered to buy the mine for a pittance. A demand that we sell that mine followed each additional incident in the mines," Rorik stated. "We've done an investigation on the mine. It turns out that your family used to own it."

"Yes," Evam agreed. "Many planetary cycles ago, my Patri's patri had lost it to your ancestors in a game of chance.

No one cared, in any case. We had mined it empty well before that," Evam explained.

"Someone cares," Daewon stated.

"Do you know anyone in your family who has said anything about it recently? "We received a ransom call a few hours ago. The kidnappers want the deed to the mine signed over to them, or my mate and child die," Rorik let that sink in for a moment.

"Solaini is the only one I can think of. She had mentioned something about it right after Rorik's accident."

"What did she say?" Calwin asked.

Evam sputtered for a few moments. "You couldn't possibly think that my little Solaini had anything to do with your issues," he replied indignantly.

"Where is she right now, Evam?" Calwin asked his old friend. Evam could hear a sense of urgency in his old friend's voice.

"She's at our summer home in Darkthorn," he stated as Daewon immediately informed the peacekeepers of the new development. "I expect to hear an apology from your family when this is over. My Solaini is not involved in this."

Rune was back in the tiny room. The big guy, Clak, had forced her out and given her the com. She only said one word but heard Rorik on the other line. She knew he would find her, but she had to do what she could to help herself until then. Another male, shorter than Clak but just as wide, dropped off her dinner, stale bread, and water and left with the morning tray. That gave Rune an idea; she hid the tray and cup under the mattress, and the following day, when Clak dropped off her bread and water, he looked for the tray.

"The other guy took it yesterday," Rune said from the corner of the mattress. She tried to look afraid of him, cowering in the corner so he wouldn't question her. The ruse worked. Clak grunted and left the room, locking the door behind him.

This routine went on a few more times until Rune figured she had enough to make a weapon. It had been two days since the call, so she knew time was running out for her rescue. Now and then, she could hear screaming coming from the floor above. Solaini's patience grew thin.

Rune jerked awake, searching for the cause. She could hear screams and grunts coming from above, along with what she thought was blaster fire. Stomping echoed down the corridor, running and stopping just outside her door. The handle turned, but this time, Rune was ready with her weapon raised behind the door. The door swung open as her arms slammed down, the collected trays hitting her captor in the face.

"Ow!" the voice shouted. Rune dropped her weapon, instantly recognizing the gravelly sound of her mate, the trays clanging unheard onto the floor.

"Rorik?" Rune whispered, unsure if her mind was playing tricks. The figure stood and growled. "Rorik!" Rune shouted this time as she launched herself into his arms. A startled "oof" sounded as strong arms wrapped around her waist. “You came for me,” she whispered into his neck. Tears streaming down her cheeks.

“Always, my sweet Rune. I will always come for you, no matter what.”

Rune suddenly gasped, “Solaini,” she started.

Rorik placed a finger on her lips. “Shh. We know. Her father told us where she was.”

“He knew?” she asked, a bit bewildered.

Rorik shook his head. “No. He refused to believe his daughter would do such a thing. He insisted on coming with us to prove us wrong.” They could hear her screams coming from outside. “How are you? Are you hurt? Of course, you are from the attack,” he asked and answered his questions. “Did she hurt you?” His hands quickly ran over every inch of Rune’s body.

“No, they didn’t hurt me. Well, Clak left some bruises when he dragged me to the com to talk to you, but that’s it.”

Rorik growled loudly, the sound reverberating deep in his chest. His hands clenched at her sides. Rune smiled at him. “I’m okay, Rorik. You saved me. I’m safe now,” she calmed her mate, running her hands up and down his biceps.

Rorik took a deep breath and nodded. “Let’s go home,” he said softly before kissing her lips, releasing all his pent-up fear and anger in that desperate kiss. When they finally broke apart, Rune swayed slightly from the lack of oxygen, and both were panting heavily. She could only nod as her lungs sought to bring in air.

Outside was chaos. Peacekeepers surrounded the building, searching for more kidnappers. Solaini fought a peacekeeper as he placed her in metal bracelets and placed her inside his land speeder. Clak and his friend lay dead off on the side of the building with several other officers standing above them. Solaini's patri spoke to another officer. His sad eyes kept going to his daughter in the speeder, still screaming and fighting to get free.

Healers arrived and took a protesting Rune to the medical center, where tests determined that Rune and the unborn child were in good health after her confinement. She was sent home with orders to rest for the next few days.

"I'm fine, Rorik, honest. The healers said to rest as a precaution. That's all," Rune argued later that night. Rorik had carried her straight to their bed from the land speeder into their home.

"I know, humor me," Rorik replied. "I need you clean and in our bed next to me," he said, carefully removing her coverings and then quickly his own.

Seeing the fear and relief in his eyes, she did as he asked. She said nothing while watching her mate draw a warm bath for her. Rorik gently carried her into the cleansing room and settled them in the tub.

Rune leaned into Rorik's chest as he soaped his hands and caressed her skin, washing away the stress and grime of the last few days. Rorik kissed her shoulders and neck, fear still coursing through his veins.

Deep lines creased his forehead. The rescue had been too close. A thousand scenarios raced through his mind at what could have been. If they had arrived a little later or his bruder hadn't figured out who was behind the attack, Rune might have been lost to him forever.

"Rorik?" Rune asked, calling him back to the present.

Shaking his head, Rorik kissed Rune's shoulder again. "Yes, my sweet Rune. I'm here."

"We've been in here quite a while now. The water is too cool, and my skin is so clean, it's puckered," Rune giggled as she held up her fingers, showing they were wrinkled.

"You're right. It would be best if you didn't catch a cold," Rorik said as he quickly stood them both and wrapped a warm towel around her body.

Scooping Rune back into his arms, he settled them into the center of the sleeping mat. Rorik held his mate close, and his eyes closed in contentment. Rune was safe, and their unborn child grew stronger every day.

"Thank you for coming for me," she quietly whispered into his chest.

"I'll always come for you, my sweet Rune. You are my life. I will cease without you by my side."

"We both could've died," Rune continued. "After the attack and then again during my rescue." Rune snuggled closer to his body. "Honestly, I don't remember much from the attack. I remember waking up in the tiny room, but I knew you would find me. I needed to be strong enough until then."

Rorik chuckled. "I couldn't believe you hit me with those trays." Rorik kissed her head. "At that moment, I was so proud of you. You were going to fight your way out of there, weren't you?" Rorik smiled again as Rune nodded slowly, her breath evening out. "Sleep, my sweet Rune. I love you," he said, kissing her head and settling in for the night, watching over his love. Hours later, Rorik's eyes finally closed, and his nightmares finally quiet.

Epilogue

"Not fair! Mama!" Rune sighed and shook her head at her youngest child. At almost five years old, her triplets were a handful. She looked across the picnic blanket at her mate playing with their oldest.

"Raine, what did Rebel do now?" she asked her youngest child by only ten minutes. Her new family and the entire planet had been shocked to discover that Rune carried triplets in her womb. Single births were the norm, twins were rare, and triplets were unheard of. Rune's mother had contacted a doctor on Earth specializing in multiple births, and Rorik had paid for the female to live on Dradus Prime for the entire pregnancy. It turned out that she also found love and decided to remain.

"I didna do noffin!" her middle child cried. His pale green eyes glistened with unshed tears. "I was playin' wif it first! She took it, an' I took it back!"

"I want it!" Raine stomped her foot and glared at her bruder. She was the miniature version of Rune, except her eyes held a tinge of brown from Rorik.

"Just because you want something doesn't make it yours. Tell Patri and Rogue that it's time to eat. You can have a turn with the toy after lunch, and once Rebel's done playing with it," Rune directed her youngest. Raine shot a dark look at her bruder before leaving to do as her majka asked.

She had just finished placing the food on the blanket when two strong arms wrapped around her bulging middle.

"Take it easy, my sweet Rune," Rorik whispered in her ear. She shivered at his voice. Even after six years, she still loved the rough sound of his voice. "Sit, Sweet Rune. I will serve you and thc children."

Rune smiled, nodded her thanks, and sat in her chair. At almost eight months along, her feet swelled continually. Growing another set of triplets, she couldn't sit comfortably on the ground, so she and Rorik sat at a small table off the side of the blanket.

"Here, Majka. Eat for you." Rogue, her oldest, handed her a plate full of food. The oldest by fifteen minutes, he was the spitting image of his Patri. He was slightly taller and bulkier than his younger bruder.

"Thank you, Rogue. You're very helpful," she praised her son. He smiled widely at her before taking his place on the blanket with his siblings.

"This is perfect, thank you," she said to Rorik as he sat down. She looked across the small meadow to the cabin where she had found the love of her life.

"Anything for you, Sweet Rune," he kissed her hand before attacking his plate. He couldn't believe how full his life had become. Six years ago, he felt sorry for himself in that cabin. The place was full of sorrow and despair. After tripling the size, it was full of love and laughter. He looked to his mate's belly and, soon, even more love.

Three years later

The Day of Choosing finally came for his oldest boys. Rorik ushered his children into the middle of a massive field filled with many eager eight-year-olds from every family in the region. Rorik sighed and looked around. He remembered his Day of Choosing and how excited and scared he had been. He looked down at his boys and saw the same wonder and awe on their faces.

"I'm doing it too, Patri," Raine declared, grabbing his hand for comfort. "I looked through the rules, and it doesn't say girls can't do it, so I want to." She looked up at him. "I don't want to stay home, Patri. I want to explore the stars like Mama did."

Rorik smiled down at his daughter. She was just as headstrong as her Majka. He didn't have the heart to tell her that the wolf-beasts gravitated more toward the males than the females. She would be heartbroken when she left the field without being chosen, but he steeled his heart from the tears that would surely come later. He looked behind them to Rune and saw that she had their youngest three, Razor, Raven, and Rooke, along the edge of the field.

"All right then, you three, wait with the others. After the Elder says the dedication, the young beasts will come to the field. Remember to keep still and wait. If the beast nuzzles your hand, they have chosen you, and you can pet them. When all beasts have chosen, the Elder will instruct you to repeat what he says to bond you to your new friend." Three heads nodded quietly.

Rorik left the field to stand beside his mate as the Elder stood on the center's high dais. "We are here for the Day of Choosing," he said. The Elder was an old, frail male, but his voice efficiently carried across the field. "Younglings, stretch out your arms and move so that no one is touching you," he instructed, waiting for everyone to finish. "Close your eyes. Open your hearts and minds, younglings, so the beasts may see what lies within you. Do not move until you are accepted, and then, only your hand may move." He looked at the nearly one hundred children scattered throughout the field. He spoke words in a language none but a select few could understand. When he said the last syllable, energy swept through the area.

Rorik watched his three oldest offspring stand amongst others on the field. His eyes followed as the different beasts stepped out of the surrounding trees. Wolf beasts were the most common, along with bird and bear beasts.

His heart went out to his daughter, knowing she most likely would not receive a companion today. Dradus Prime was a male-dominated world where the males worked outside the family house, and the females tended to stay home. Therefore, a female had no reason to have a companion to protect them.

Raine was every bit as adventurous as her bruders. His mate insisted that she be allowed the same opportunities as her siblings. Rorik's chest swelled with pride as he observed her stand confidently among her peers. His heart ached at the slight tremble on her lips.

A hushed gasp swept across the families on the outer edges of the field. A nebari, a rare beast that hadn't been seen in over two hundred planetary cycles, strolled among the younglings. Nebaries were solitary, feline beasts that tended to ignore all other creatures. When they did find a companion, they were highly possessive. A fully grown Nebari stood taller than a wolf beast, and their large canine teeth protruded from their upper jaw even with their mouths closed.

The nebari closed in on its intended target. Rorik's heart drummed in his ears as it stopped before his baby girl. The animal licked her hand and waited. Raine kept her eyes closed but extended her hand to pet the beast's head. The animal purred and rubbed up against her.

The Elder spoke again in the magical language, the children repeated, and the ritual was complete. Every child on the field walked away with a bonded companion.

Rune regarded her oldest children nervously as they raced to her with their new companions. She was unsure what had happened, but the audience's reaction to this Choosing told her something significant had occurred. She would interrogate her mate later on, back at home.

"Mama! I have a new companion!" her middle child rushed toward her, a wolf-beast by his side. "This is Eoho, and he's my new best friend!" Rune smiled at her son and then welcomed Eoho into the family.

Rogue calmly stood beside his bruder and rolled his eyes with the superiority only an older sibling could get away with. "Majka, Patri, this is Tack, my new companion." Rune again welcomed the wolf-beast into the family.

Rune looked around to find Raine, but she was nowhere around. A roar filled the air, causing people to shriek in fear. With Rorik by her side, Rune fought through the crowd to find their daughter surrounded by adults trying to grab at the nebari.

"Quiet!" Rorik shouted. Silence descended on the crowd as all eyes turned toward them. "Leave my child alone!" he growled.

"Patri, I would like to introduce you and Mama to my new companion, Jinx," Raine said calmly, ignoring the crowd surrounding them.

"Females shouldn't receive companions!" an angry bystander shouted.

"My son should get the nebari. He deserves it more than a female!" another shouted.

Before Rorik or Rune could respond, the crowd parted for the Elder. He approached Raine and Jinx, then bowed low to show respect to the beast. Jinx lowered her head to acknowledge him before he spoke to the crowd. "As you all know, the beast chooses the child. It is the child's choice to enter into the Choosing or not. Male or Female, all are welcome to enter," he stressed the word female.

The Elder raised his hand to stop the arguments from erupting around him. "The nebari has chosen; the ritual is now complete. There is nothing any of you can do about it. I command you to leave this family alone."

Another five years later

Rune and Rorik again stood at the edge of the field. Their youngest children were already on the field. They had refused help from their parents, remembering what to do from watching their older siblings' years before.

A new Elder, who was just as frail-looking, stood on the dais. Rorik smiled with pride at his offspring. Since Raine had entered the Choosing, more females had entered each year, effectively altering the future workforce. More and more females were choosing to work outside the home, necessitating the need for a companion. Some children, male and female alike, walk away without a companion, but those times are few.

Rune waited with bated breath and crossed her fingers. She prayed to the Old Gods that her children would receive a companion. The beasts approached the field, and one by one, the animals chose. When it was over, and the Elder spoke the final words, Rune was white with shock. She had expected more wolf-beasts. That was not what chose her babies.

"Mama! Patri! I want to introduce you to my new friend!" "This is Coal," her daughter Raven, the oldest of the triplets, said. She introduced them to a giant bird. The biggest Rune had ever seen. Its feathers were so black; they shone with a kaleidoscope of colors.

As she had done before, Rune welcomed the animal into the family. "It looks like you will be getting a larger room, my daughter," Rorik said with a smile. "A full-grown bird-beast has a wingspan equal to the length of our home."

Rune stared in shock at her mate. "Our home is over fifty feet long!" Rorik just laughed at her expression.

"Majka, Patri, this is Artan," her youngest son and the youngest triplet, Razor, said. He introduced a bear-beast cub that was the same size as him. Again, Rune welcomed him into the family.

"My turn," announced her youngest daughter. "This is Moki. She's a Koro," Rooke introduced a giant ape-like creature as her new companion.

Rorik held his mate in a tight embrace, easing the distressed look on her face. "It seems our three youngest children will be getting larger rooms," he chuckled. "One thing for certain, my love," he sighed. "Our lives will never be boring."

www.ingramcontent.com/pod-product-compliance
Lightning Source LLC
LaVergne TN
LVHW010931110826
845149LV00013B/2541

9781964030838